She stood with her hands on her hips.

"So this is…" she glanced up into the rafters as if the word for whatever *this* was hid among them "…a bit weird, I know."

A bit weird? Bo managed what he hoped looked like a calm shrug. "Doesn't have to be." It became immediately apparent that wasn't the best choice of response.

"But it does have to be professional. I just want to be clear this is a business relationship. Clear boundaries."

So she'd been worrying about this, too. The knowledge of her anxiety over how their mutual history could cloud things over only sharpened his radar. After all, she was the one who called him.

"Absolutely," he agreed, because it seemed the safest thing to say.

Toni crossed her arms over her chest. "No extras, no cozy chats, no 'remember whens.'"

She wasn't drawing boundaries, she was throwing up twenty-foot walls. Given how much time together this job would take, would that even work?

Allie Pleiter, an award-winning author and RITA® Award finalist, writes both fiction and nonfiction. Her passion for knitting shows up in many of her books and all over her life. Entirely too fond of French macarons and lemon meringue pie, Allie spends her days writing books and avoiding housework. Allie grew up in Connecticut, holds a BS in speech from Northwestern University and lives near Chicago, Illinois.

Books by Allie Pleiter

Love Inspired

Wander Canyon

Their Wander Canyon Wish
Winning Back Her Heart

Matrimony Valley

His Surprise Son
Snowbound with the Best Man
Wander Canyon Courtship

Blue Thorn Ranch

The Texas Rancher's Return
Coming Home to Texas
The Texan's Second Chance
The Bull Rider's Homecoming
The Texas Rancher's New Family

Visit the Author Profile page at Harlequin.com for more titles.

Winning Back Her Heart

Allie Pleiter

Recycling programs for this product may not exist in your area.

ISBN-13: 978-1-335-48815-2

Winning Back Her Heart

This is a work of fiction. Names, characters, places and incidents are either the product of the author's imagination or are used fictitiously. Any resemblance to actual persons, living or dead, businesses, companies, events or locales is entirely coincidental.

This edition published by arrangement with Harlequin Books S.A.

For questions and comments about the quality of this book, please contact us at CustomerService@Harlequin.com.

Love Inspired
22 Adelaide St. West, 40th Floor
Toronto, Ontario M5H 4E3, Canada
www.Harlequin.com

Printed in U.S.A.

And I will restore to you
the years that the locust hath eaten.
—*Joel* 2:25

To the unseen rebuilders everywhere—
those who quietly shore up homes,
buildings, hearts and lives.

Chapter One

Despite his every effort not to, Bo Carter found himself parked on Main Street staring at the blue-and-white awning of Redding's General Store. Toni Redding was back in Wander Canyon for the weekend, inside that store.

Get it over with, he told himself. *You can't avoid seeing her.* The Colorado town he called home didn't have enough places to hide. Certainly not when half the town knew his history with Toni. Wander being the small-town gossipfest that it was, Bo could think of six people off the top of his head who might contrive a meeting just to see if they'd yell or hug the first time he and Toni saw each other.

He didn't know which he'd do, either.

Bo watched the store lights flick off and the two lantern-style lights on either side of the big red wooden door come on. Bo didn't need to check his watch to know Toni's father, Don, was closing up for the night. Redding's closed at 5:30 p.m. every night like clockwork. He saw the old man reaching up to flip the Open sign to Closed the same way he'd watched Don do it for years. How many long-ago evenings had he sat on the bench outside the shop waiting for Toni to be done behind the register so they could go to the movies or grab a pizza? It had to be hundreds. It felt like twice that.

How many hours had he and Toni spent on that bench? Laughing, holding hands, making up all kinds of silly dreams about what life would be like after high school. Pretending that they were meant to be together forever.

This is a bad idea. You're not ready to see her. Go someplace—anyplace—else. Bo knew the smart thing to do would be to drive off when Don shuffled out the door. He shifted his truck out of Neutral. Any street in Wander Canyon would be safer for him than where he was right now.

Still, when he caught sight of the particular shade of red that was Toni's hair—a color he figured would never leave his memory—he froze. The ridiculous belief that if he stayed still she wouldn't see him pinned him to his seat. Impossible, since the truck door panel directly below his window read Car-San Construction. Toni knew he'd launched this business with his high school buddy Jake. She'd know it was his truck.

She'd know it was him.

It happened just like he knew it would. The air changed when she came into view. The crazy curls of her red hair had softened to sophisticated waves, but he'd know those dimples anywhere. She had a big-city polish about her that was poised and beautiful.

He, on the other hand, was as grimy and rugged as he was after any long day at his construction business. Why didn't he choose a time when he was clean and showered and ready? *Because you'd never be ready, that's why.*

He knew the moment she saw him. She stopped helping her dad, frozen by the sight of him even though he was clear across the street. Bo had the odd sensation that he could have been standing halfway across the canyon and she'd have seen him.

He had hurt Toni. Badly. He'd always known that, but in this moment he knew it down to his bones. Her eyes told him so. He'd made the choice back then to end things badly—cowardly on his part, but his pride had tangled his sense, convincing him it would hurt less to let her leave if she hated him. He couldn't have stood knowing she had walked away still loving him.

But it had hurt either way. It hurt like an avalanche roaring through him, taking down everything in its path. And as he caught the ice in her eyes just now, the wound ripped wide-open, as if she'd said goodbye yesterday.

He forced himself to breathe when Toni said something to her father and headed toward him as Mr. Redding made his way over to the bench in front of the store.

A wordless gulp of a prayer, something along the lines of *Lord, please let me not be a jerk*, rose up as Bo turned off the ignition.

Toni was a beauty, still, but there was something new about her he couldn't quite name. A strength? A grace? Confidence? Whatever it was, it made her twice as gorgeous, and Bo felt his pulse rise as she came closer.

"Hello, Bo." That voice. She'd always had a silky alto, but somehow it had deepened and become even more smooth. This was a bad idea. He should have gone straight home.

"Toni." He couldn't quite figure out what else to say.

She exhaled and shifted her weight. "I figured I was going to bump into you at some point."

He scrambled for some shred of conversation. "I'd heard you were back for Mari's bridal shower. And the wedding in a couple of weeks." He tried to shrug. "Wyatt Walker. I didn't see that one coming."

She gave a tense laugh. In truth, the unlikely pairing of local rebel Wyatt Walker with the sweet mother of young twins really did raise a few local eyebrows. "I know, but Mari's really happy. She's had a rough go of it, so I'm glad for her, you know?"

"Yeah." Being widowed at a young age was tragic enough, but Mari Sofitel had been betrayed by her late husband and left alone with twin daughters. It had been the talk of town for a while.

"I had ideas," Toni said, "about what I'd do when I saw you again."

"Like maybe a good solid slap across my face?" he joked, then regretted it instantly. It was a stupid thing to say. He hadn't expected her to unnerve him quite this badly.

"As a matter of fact..." she began. "Not that I would." She looked back over her shoulder at her father, and for a split second they were teenagers again, vying for time under a parent's watchful eye.

"I'd deserve it." He would. There were a hundred

better ways to part with Toni than what he'd chosen. Being eighteen and heartbroken didn't excuse the jerk he'd made of himself that fall. He should say something mature and heartfelt. The only thing he could manage was "How are you?"

That softened her. Not a lot, but a bit. "I'm good." She cast her glance back over her shoulder again. "Worried about Dad, I suppose."

"Don? He'll go on forever." Which wasn't true. He looked at Don as he sat on the bench. It was as if someone had peeled a film off his vision and he could see how the man had aged since Toni's mom, Irene, had died. The slump of his shoulders, the way he leaned on a cane with the weariness of someone well beyond his years. The store needed a paint job and a hundred other repairs. Irene used to sweep off the sidewalk in front of the store every morning, but no one did that anymore. Hadn't Hank Walker at church said Don had been having health issues?

"I…um…well, I suppose you should hear it from me." Toni twirled a strand of hair around one finger the way she always did when she was nervous. "I'm back."

"Well, sure," he replied. "For the shower and the wedding and all."

She shifted her weight again. "No, I mean I'm coming back. For good."

Toni watched Bo take in the dramatic declaration she'd just made. The decision to stay in Wander was minutes old—or months, it was hard to say. The sensation that she was approaching a tipping point in her life had filled her since she got off the plane this morning. Spending the afternoon with Dad at the store, she'd been startled by the state of his health and the decline of the business that had been her family's whole life.

Within those few hours, the realization crystallized: she wasn't back just for a visit. She was coming home for good. Sure, it was sudden, but this wasn't impulsive. It was decisive, and that was a different thing entirely.

Still, this moment was the first time she'd said it out loud. And to Bo Carter, of all people.

He looked stunned. He had every right to. It was a stunning moment.

"I'm moving back to Wander," she repeated, almost more for herself than Bo. It should have felt like an enormous pronouncement, a whiplash turn of events, only it didn't. Even if her motivations were still a bit on the fuzzy side, her words felt like this was the right thing to do. "I'm going to run the store. I'm going to turn it into my version of Redding's so Dad can retire."

The only catch was that Dad didn't know. Yet.

Surprise raised Bo's eyebrows. "Wow. He must be happy about that." He'd always had a gift for saying either the right thing or the thing to pull the rug out from under her. Clearly, he still had that gift.

Toni felt her face redden and a new wave of uncertainty wash over her. "Well, no," she stammered. "Because he doesn't actually know. Well, not yet, anyways."

Bo's face took on the "you gotta be kidding me" expression she knew so well from high school. "Don doesn't know?"

Coming home to Wander Canyon and taking over

Redding's was the solution to all the questions and frustrations that had been piling up for the last two months in New York. For the last year of nearly buckling under the pressure of working for someone as impossible as Faye Collins.

Of course, there was the little matter of *how*, but she'd figure that out. While loads of people had gotten themselves fired, no one dared quit on Faye Collins. It just wasn't done. Still, God would clear a path if it really was the right thing to do, wouldn't He?

Toni planted her hands on her hips. "I've only just now decided."

Bo's deep brown eyes gave her a "tell me more" gaze that could always render her defenseless. "How recently 'just now'?"

"About thirty minutes ago." She straightened her spine and added, "But I've been thinking about it for weeks. Months, actually."

His expression shifted and warmed. Bo chose his words carefully, and it unnerved her that he seemed to sense how fragile an idea this was for her. "I've always thought you were born to run the place. And not just because your last name is Redding." He shifted his hands on the truck steering wheel, and she noticed the scar on the back of his hand that he'd gotten when they went fishing once. There was *so much* history between them. It made it hard to know how to act, what to say. "So I take it New York is not so great anymore?"

How had he summed it up in such simple terms? The reasons why she was ready to leave were a four-hour conversation, not an exchange of words on the sidewalk while Dad was waiting. "You could say that."

"Or is it on account of Don?"

"Little bit of both." Dad might be the reason she was ready to come home, but Faye was a big part of the reason she was ready to leave New York.

She'd grown disillusioned with Faye Collins and her job at Hearth Homegoods. Being Faye's personal assistant had been the job of a lifetime, but it had consumed her whole life. She no longer loved her work. The prestige of scoring the assistant position straight out of college, of being considered Faye Collins's protégée, had swept her up at first. It was dazzling to be taken in by someone so influential and important. But in the past year, it had become exhausting and overwhelming.

"It's just... Well, there are some things I want to do that I think I can only do here." There were things about the Colorado mountains, the lifestyle here that she'd come to realize were the core of who she was. Faye had taken her in like a daughter, filled the aching hole that had been left when Mom died. But Faye had also changed her into someone else, and Toni couldn't ever remember agreeing to that.

Bo didn't offer a response, and the stretch of silence between them felt prickly and awkward. Each of them fidgeted, grappling with the idea of her permanent return. They'd see each other like this often now. Wander Canyon wasn't so big that they could hope to avoid regular encounters. Toni hoped it would get better as time went on, because right now it felt awful.

"Can you not say anything? To anyone yet?" Toni felt

her face redden again. "I'm not even sure why I just told you. I mean, before I told Dad. What's up with that?"

Her question pricked something in Bo's eyes. The hard truth that maybe, while they had loads of history, they couldn't be close, not after what he'd done. It stung way deep down in her chest, a long tamped-down wound that sprang open again at the sight of him.

She'd worked so hard to make their parting sweet and friendly, and he'd gone and turned it into something awful. She'd tenderly kissed him goodbye that night on the very bench where Dad now sat. Bo had driven her home to sleep her last night in town before getting on a plane to design school and a new life in New York City.

She'd been sad to end it, of course, but proud of how they put an honorable sort of closure on the different direction their lives were taking.

But Bo had gone out later that night and made a total mess of himself. The stories reached her quickly: half a dozen girls, months of carousing, a wrecked car and enough wild behavior that he only barely escaped landing up in jail. "A total train wreck," Mari had called it. What's worse, people were woefully quick to decide she'd driven him to it. As if the wild boy he became was somehow her fault.

"I won't say anything." Bo's reply snapped her back to the present. His words had the air of an apology. Still, anything he did now could never make up for what he'd done that night. And those months after. He'd made her feel like a heartbreaking snob, as if she were cruelly discarding him and all of Wander in her grand plans to show New York what a mountain girl was made of.

"I appreciate that." She used to be able to tell Bo anything. He could pull the most private dreams and wishes and fears out of her. Perhaps he knew more about her way down deep inside than anyone else on the planet.

But the six years she'd been gone had changed them both. Up until this second, she'd viewed revamping Redding's as a giant leap forward. Looking at Bo, feeling the whirlwind of emotions spinning in her at the moment, it suddenly began to feel like a dangerous falling back.

That's not true, she told herself. *Decisive, not impulsive. This is what you want. What Dad needs. Be strong enough to go for it.*

"You look great," he offered a bit sheepishly, as if he wasn't sure that was okay to say.

Toni didn't know how to respond. The years had sat well on him, too. He was still fit and handsome, with a touch of a boy's mussy hair but a man's hint of dark brown stubble on his angled features. In many ways she'd left a boy behind in Wander and was now looking at a man. One who still had brown eyes that could sparkle light or simmer dark, and a smile that could undo her in a second.

She'd purposely not kept up on his life. Mari would occasionally drop a fact here and there, but not much more. She knew he was still single and that he'd gone into business with Jake.

Bo glanced over her shoulder to where Dad was sitting. "I should probably let you go."

"Yeah." Toni wanted to whack her forehead at the

ridiculous small talk they could only seem to manage despite all their history. She shrugged and turned to go.

"Hey," he said as she took her first steps back across the street. She turned around to see that smile, just as disarming as it had always been. "That wasn't as bad as I thought it'd be."

"What?"

"Seeing you again. A little rough, but we powered through." He used to say that about football practice, or chemistry exams, or when he got his wisdom teeth out.

"I suppose."

No, it wasn't as bad as she'd thought it would be.

It was worse.

Chapter Two

"So that's what I want to do with Redding's." Toni swallowed hard after she laid out her plans for the store to her father after dinner.

Mom and Dad had always stood behind her. She'd been amazed how Dad had encouraged her decision to move to New York. Even when it left him alone in Wander Canyon, since her mother had died just over a year before. "It's what your mother would have wanted," he'd said. Would Mom have approved of the proposal she'd made just now?

Dad didn't answer right away, and it made Toni's stomach tumble in doubt. What she'd just proposed to him couldn't have come as anything but a shock. He had likely toyed with the idea of her taking over the store at some point. Only what she'd just outlined wasn't just a takeover. It was a complete overhaul of Redding's into something entirely new.

"It's different," Dad said. His tone wasn't quite enthusiastic.

"It is," Toni replied. This was the answer—she knew it in her bones. "And it's a lot to take in, I know. But Dad, I really think this could be the future—*my* future *here*—with Redding's." She saw a flicker of curiosity fill his eyes, along with the startled disbelief that his daughter might actually be coming home to stay.

She could also see what she'd hoped to find in his expression: relief. He might not be ready to admit out loud that the store was too much for him, but they both knew it.

"You've been holding down the store for years without Mom." The last two words caught thickly in her throat. "You deserve to take it easy," Toni went on. "I want to do this. For you, and for me." She felt her voice catch a bit. "I don't belong in New York anymore. I belong here."

Dad's eyes glistened. "I never liked you living so far away. But..." His words trailed off. Redding's had been his life, the thing he'd built from the ground up with Mom. Asking to change the store felt like asking to change their legacy. Was that brave? Or disrespectful?

Dad gave a shaky little sigh. "It sounds awfully newfangled."

Toni smiled at the old-fashioned word to describe the new Redding's. She made the decision right then and there to use "newfangled" in her marketing. "That's exactly what it is, Dad." New, but rooted in the old. Unstuffy but not behind the times.

"It'll be a big job, won't it? All by yourself?" It was the closest Dad had come to admitting just how far the physical state of the store had slipped in recent years.

"Well, yes. But with the right people and all the work I plan to put into it, I don't think it will take too long. I'll start right away, and we might be able to manage a grand reopening for the third of July." The Redding's Third of July Sale was a Wander Canyon tradition, so linking the reopening to the sale helped Redding's keep its roots while spreading new wings.

Dad's eyes widened. "You'll close the store for renovations?" Redding's had never closed, even during blizzards or any other number of disasters. It had been a point of family pride that anyone could get what they needed at Redding's any day of the year—except, of course, Sundays and major holidays. Mom and Dad had never opened the store on the Lord's day.

Toni had anticipated this reaction from her father. "Not completely. I think we can keep about half of the store open while we work. We'd just have to section off the parts where construction would make it unsafe for customers."

"Gotta keep it safe." He was coming around to the idea, she could see.

"I want everyone to see the work happening, to watch the transformation take place." The more she spoke about it, the more the dream anchored to her soul. Toni hadn't even realized how much energy her life had lost until she felt it rekindle.

She held her father's gaze for a moment, then summoned up her courage to ask, "What do you think?"

There was a nerve-racking pause as Dad looked at his hands. It was foolish to think he'd jump on the bandwagon right away—the store was his life's work. He'd never done anything else, hardly ever taken a day off since Mom died. Handing Redding's over to her represented a huge change in both their lives. Toni had the dizzying sense of Redding family history hinging on this moment.

Two weeks ago, as she watched her evenings and weekends disappear behind a long list of tasks Faye had given her, she could have never predicted life would have brought her to this moment. Now, she was on the brink of stepping into the future God had waiting all along—or so she hoped.

Dad's smile was bittersweet as he squeezed Toni's hand. "I guess newfangled sounds like it could be dandy."

Dandy. There wasn't a word that captured Dad better than that. "Yeah, it could."

Toni watched a little sparkle of acceptance come to his blue eyes. She had her father's chin and his height, but she'd gotten Mom's bright green eyes and slightly unruly cascade of red hair. Growing up, Toni had been annoyed at how easily she was marked as Irene Redding's daughter. Now she loved having a bit of her mother with her always.

"I suppose," he said slowly, "it might be fun to take up fishing again. Haven't had much time for that."

"You deserve to do all the fishing you want." The glimpses of fragility she'd seen in her father gave the words a tender weight. *How much time for fishing does he have left?* He shouldn't spend his golden years minding the store.

Toni got off the couch and sat next to him. "Please, Dad. Let me do this. For me, and for you."

The laughter and hugging—and perhaps a few tears—that followed his nod felt like the world shifting and laying itself open before her.

She wasn't just coming home—she was coming home to become who she was always meant to be.

Bo barely remembered any of the drive home. The ache in his chest seemed to swallow him whole, and he drove home on sheer muscle memory.

There were a million things he should have done when he got back to his apartment. Ordinary tasks to yank him out of the fog Toni had plunged him into. He should have eaten. Fed and walked his dog, Dodger. Opened the mail. Answered the call from his sister, Peggy about having breakfast tomorrow. At least tossed a ball in the patient beagle's direction.

He hadn't done any of those things. Instead, Bo stood in his backyard and stared off into the mountains, barely even noticing Dodger's pleas for attention at his feet.

The voice of his friend and business partner, Jake Sanders, came from behind him. "You did it, didn't you?" He'd been so lost in the storm of his thoughts that he hadn't even heard Jake's truck come up the drive.

"Did what?" The low angle of the sun made him wonder how long he'd been standing there. An hour? Ten minutes?

Jake rolled his eyes. "Went and saw her." He leaned down and scratched Dodger behind the ears.

"Did you follow me or something?"

"Didn't have to. The way you looked at the end of

the day gave you away easy. Plus, Redding's is in the opposite direction of here, and I saw you leave."

"Okay, so, yes, I went to the store and saw her." Bo held on to the slim hope that Jake would let it go at that.

Of course, he didn't. "I don't like the look in your eyes, buddy. She *left*, Bo. She left *you*. You can't really still have a thing for her, can you?"

"No." Who was he kidding? "Maybe."

Jake walked over to the bucket of tennis balls beside the back door and lobbed one halfway across the yard. Jake hadn't been Wander High's star pitcher for no reason. He eyed Bo as Dodger lumbered off after the ball, thrilled for someone to finally be playing with him. "That's insane. You know that, right? You have plans you're about to kick into gear. August. Florida. Your folks." After years of working together, he and Jake were making plans to open two Car-San locations—Jake running a business up here in Colorado while Bo opened another down in Florida, ready to help his parents and the loads of other people who needed to rebuild during and after hurricane season.

Toni Redding's return to town shouldn't affect those plans one bit. That would be the logical way to look at it. But since when was anything he thought or felt about Toni Redding logical?

"Don't, man." Jake cautioned when Bo didn't answer. "Don't even think it. We've almost got the split all set up and ready to go." While they were technically running two arms of the same business, Jake always referred to their next move as "the split."

"Besides, I'm in no mood to scrape you up off the

sidewalk again. She's here for a week, tops. A couple of days for the shower and a couple of days for the wedding. You can power through that, right?"

If only that were true. She was here for good, back in Wander, if not back in his life, but he'd promised Toni not to say anything. Her return pummeled him with an excruciating blend of terror and optimism that spun his insides like a cement mixer.

"Look, you got the hard part over with. You came, you saw, you did the awkward chat thing, you got the worst of it over."

Oh, it is so far from over. I don't know what it is, but over isn't it.

Jake grabbed Bo's shoulder. He got the sense Jake was tamping down the urge to shake him. He'd earned his friend's annoyance—Jake's remark about scraping Bo up off the sidewalk wasn't much of an exaggeration. "If you can't shake her, then make yourself scarce. Head down to your folks' in Florida now instead of in August. I'll hire a couple of guys and finish up our summer projects without you."

"You can't do that..."

"I can. And believe me, I'd rather do that than watch you go under again."

Bo had originally agreed to spend the slower winter season down in Florida helping his parents rebuild from the hurricane that had damaged their house. But he and Jake were turning it into more than that. They were going to leverage the advantages of both locations. And Bo knew that the minute he disclosed his plans to take up permanent residence in Florida, Mom and Dad and Peggy would jump on it as the solution to worrying about Mom and Dad. Because it was.

"Rebuild your parents' dock so fast you fall into bed exhausted at night," Jake pressed. "Then rebuild their garage. And their porch. And the neighbor's porch. Rebuild the entire subdivision if that's what it takes to get Toni out of your system."

He could rebuild Mom and Dad's house from the foundation up—and a dozen others beside—and it wouldn't be enough. The truth was that despite thousands of miles and six years' time, he'd never really let go of Toni. He'd measured every woman he'd ever dated—and there weren't that many of them, as Jake often reminded him—against Toni. Even after how much she'd hurt him.

"It won't help."

"Sure it will," Jake persisted. "Sunshine, Florida beaches..." Bo watched his friend's eyes take on a worried look. "You can't let a little visit from her take you under like this."

"She's staying." Bo justified the small betrayal by telling himself he'd only promised not to say anything to Toni's father.

Jake froze at that. "She's what?"

"Toni's moving back to Wander." It wasn't fair what those words did to his insides. "No one knows yet."

"But you do."

"It slipped out while we were talking."

Pinching the bridge of his nose, Jake made a frustrated sound. "So Toni Redding is back in town. For good."

"That's about the gist of it."

Jake fixed Bo with a somber glare. "Leave tomorrow morning. I'll take you to the airport myself, man. 'Cause if you don't, you're toast."

New cash register system.
New floor plan.
New shelving.
New lighting.
Refinished floors.

That night Toni looked at her to-do list—her *very long* to-do list—and thought she'd have to win every lottery in Colorado to finance all the repairs to Redding's that were needed. Either that, or invest a whopping load of elbow grease.

Only it would take way more than elbow grease and determination to get Redding's back up to speed. It would take skills and expertise way beyond what she had. She needed a contractor, and a great one at that.

Her heart sank when an internet search brought up only one local company: Bo's. She'd already decided every aspect of this overhaul would have to be done as locally as possible. The newfangled Redding's had to be homegrown. But using Bo?

On the upside, he seemed to have earned the respect of many people in Wander while she was gone. While it might be a mountain of awkward, she'd get an honest price and fair work out of Bo and his partner.

But doing a big job fast and frugal meant she would be logging in long hours alongside Bo. That was a shaky prospect at best. Or an invitation to the world's longest emotional baggage–laden argument at worst.

If she chose Bo, this would either go very well…or very badly.

She clicked over to the Car-San website from the listing, nearly laughing at the friendly photo of Bo and Jake grinning in front of their truck. Contractors You Can Trust, the caption said.

"Can I trust you to be a grown-up about this?" she asked the image out loud. "Keep things on a professional level? You can be too charming." She scowled at Bo's image. "And I'm in a bit of a shaky place at the moment."

The new Redding's needed to be locally sourced. Her vision included goods and crafts and art from people right here in the canyon or nearby. The plain truth was that if she gave the renovation job to someone outside the canyon, it would undercut that vision from the start.

There was nothing for it. She had to at least give him a chance to bid on the project. Inhaling a deep breath of clear mountain air—something that still felt like a spectacular privilege after so much New York City grime—Toni typed an email to Car-San Construction asking Bo to meet her at the shop tomorrow.

He could be too busy to take this on, right, Lord? she prayed, even though she knew Bo was the kind of person who would make time to help her out. *I'll take this step, but I'm going to leave the outcome up to You. Nobody else knows if this is a great opportunity or a giant mistake.*

The answer came in seven minutes. "For you, I'll find the time."

Chapter Three

Peggy gave Bo one of her sisterly looks over coffee and muffins at the Wander Canyon Bakery early the next morning. Peggy's husband, Carl, was the high school track coach, so mornings were the best time for her to grab a moment away while her two young boys were in school.

"So," she began in a parental "let's have a discussion" tone, "you know what weekend it is?"

That was the trouble with older sisters. They never let you get away with anything. "Wow. You made it halfway through your muffin before you brought it up. I figured you would start in the moment we sat down." He bit into the flaky egg-and-cheese sandwich that made for a heartier breakfast than his usual choice of a bear claw or a muffin. Today he was going to need fortification. Come to think of it, he was going to need fortification for this current conversation.

"Have you seen her yet?"

Seen her? I might be working with her. "We bumped into each other yesterday."

"And how was that?"

"It wasn't as awful as I thought it might be." That was true. Sort of. To say he and Toni hadn't left off on the best of terms was an understatement. Sure, they'd been head over heels for each other in high school and the summer after, but he should have known how it would end. Toni had always been heading in a different direction than him.

College? New York City? That would never be him, and the strength of what he felt for her would never have been enough to make that work.

Just like what she'd felt for him wasn't enough to make her stay.

Peggy cleared her throat, and he realized his thoughts had wandered. Again. His concentration had been shot since the moment he'd heard Toni was coming to town. Maybe Jake was right and the only thing for it was to get out of Wander pronto. And permanently, now that she was staying. Of course, that flew in the face of the meeting he was about to go to after breakfast.

"Well, at least she's only here for this weekend and then for the wedding."

"Actually..." Bo began, almost wincing at how he knew Peggy would respond to the news he was about to share. Toni had mentioned in her email that she'd gotten her father's agreement to overhaul the store, which meant he wasn't bound to his promise of silence anymore.

His sister's eyes narrowed. "Actually what?"

"She's taking over the store so that Don can retire."

Peggy's expression was a combination of protective and suspicious. "And you know all this how?"

She'd find out soon enough—better Peggy heard it from him than from someone else. "She's asked me to bid on doing the work on the store."

"You said no, right? I mean, you can't if you're going down to Mom and Dad's."

"I can do it and finish before August. I'm heading over there after this to talk to her about it."

Peggy practically dropped her muffin. "Why on earth would you do that?"

"She asked me to bid on the project. How would it look if I just turned her down without talking to her?"

Peggy sat back. "Like you had a bone of sense in your body." Mom shouldn't worry one bit whether he was being mothered while his parents were in Florida. Peggy was filling that role just fine, even if he was twenty-five and didn't need it.

"It could be an important job for Car-San. I get that the timing—and the customer—are a bit tricky." He tried a diversionary tactic. "But it's not a social thing. I'm not even invited to the wedding, so I won't see her outside of work. If I take the job." Peggy and Carl were friends with Marilyn Sofitel's parents, so they were invited, but Bo wasn't surprised at all to be off the wedding invitation list. He was relieved, in fact.

Peggy would not be diverted. "So come up with another reason to turn it down. We can make up some reason you had to head down to Florida early." Her eyes softened. “Mom and Dad need your help, and you certainly don’t need to be here.”

“I can’t just leave Jake hanging,” he fibbed. “We have a bunch of jobs to finish up before the fall.” That wasn’t quite true. In fact, there wasn’t much at all stopping him from heading down south as soon as he wanted to. Not that he’d ever tell Peggy that.

“I’ll work on Jake,” Peggy offered. She’d always been a champion meddler.

“Don’t. Just let me work this out on my own, okay?” A huge part of him wanted to see if he could use this job to make things right with Toni. To put right the one thing that had felt out of order in his life for years. And what he’d said about the timing was true. If she really wanted the quick timetable she mentioned in her email, he could do the job, put a better ending on the sad story of their relationship and head to Florida before Labor Day with a clear conscience and a bit more money in the Car-San coffers. It wouldn’t be easy, but maybe he owed it to himself—and Toni—to try.

Peggy leaned in, concern filling her features. “I think it’s a bad idea. You were a mess when Toni left the last time. I don’t want to see you back there.”

“You and Jake both.” He tried to put into words the tangle of emotions Toni’s return had brought up. “I’ll admit, it still stings…to see her, I mean.” Maybe the hurt would soften into the “it was for the best” kind of hurt, but yesterday felt much more like the “girl that got away” kind.

He was glad Peggy didn’t ask him, “Are you over her?” because he didn’t have an answer.

She touched his shoulder. "Be careful, Bo."

"I'll have to be, won't I?"

But could he be?

The truth was that he'd never really gotten over Toni Redding. And the trouble with this job was that it stood the very real chance of pulling that heartbreak out and letting it shred him from the inside all over again.

This is a second chance to put the right ending on everything.

At least that's what Bo told himself as he walked the short distance down Wander Canyon's Main Street from the bakery to Redding's General Store. He believed Toni's arrival back in town wasn't just coincidence. He wanted to believe that God had opened a door for redemption with her.

Of course, it was just as likely this job would give him a second chance to wreck it all. Toni could make him crazy in ways no woman ever had or probably ever would. He'd never been able to shake the belief that they belonged together. Her being back here, needing something from him, now…there had to be a reason for it. At the very least, he could show her that the man he'd become wasn't the same boy she'd left years ago.

Play it cool, he told himself. *Keep it professional.* He'd half considered bringing Jake with him, but Jake's lack of tact was too much of a minefield in this particular circumstance. No, this meeting was best kept between himself and Toni.

Their long history seemed to hang in the air between them as Toni pulled open the store's front door.

"Right on time," she said, one eyebrow raised in slight amusement. He hadn't exactly been known for punctuality back in the day. "And with coffee, too."

As an extra olive branch, Bo had brought coffee from the Wander Canyon Bakery—cream and two sugars for hers. He knew how she took her coffee, just as she knew his favorite pizza came from Cuccio's down on Garden Avenue. *So much history.*

"I was having breakfast with Peggy," he explained, not wanting it to look like he'd gone out of his way to please her.

"How is your sister?" Bo took it as a good sign that she asked about his family.

"Great. She has two five-year-old boys now." He shrugged. "Just call me Uncle Bo."

Toni offered a smile at that but seemed to shut it down quickly. She straightened her shoulders. "Where do you want to start?" He didn't know how to react to the slight touch of unsteadiness in her voice. It was understandable, he supposed, given the amount of raw ground between them. Most—but not all—of that was his doing. It wasn't going to be crossed overnight. He wasn't sure it could be crossed at all.

"Anywhere you want. I'm ready if you are." If he knew Toni—and he did—she'd have the entire renovation all planned out in her head already, with a long list of details. Probably even sketches. It was best to let her run this meeting.

She led him through the cluttered aisles toward the back of the store. "I'm afraid it's going to be a big job. There's a lot I want to do." Even though uncertainty clipped the edges of her words, Toni's voice had gained a depth and texture that suited her.

"I like a challenge."

They arrived at a table strewn with papers and sketches. "It's important to me that everything stays as local as possible. Vendors, supplies, materials—I want to keep Redding's a Wander icon."

Bo forced his attention to her detailed notes as she walked him through the long list of upgrades and renovations she had in mind. It was a clever mix of modern technology and convenience wrapped up in the classic, rustic Redding's atmosphere. Brand-new lighting sunk into old and weathered wood. Video screens framed in barn wood and gingham. New electric and Wi-Fi. She was knocking down the store's current maze of narrow aisles in favor of an open floor plan.

"I want it to feel as if my customers are walking into a favorite aunt's country kitchen." Her eyes sparkled with excitement when she said *my customers*. He was right—she'd been born to do this. He'd half expected her to open a store after she went off to that fancy New York school. But then again, he'd expected a lot of things of Toni Redding that hadn't happened. So what made her not just come home, but *move* home now? Today definitely wasn't the time to get into that conversation.

"New logo, too?" he asked, pointing to a set of sketched designs that made use of Redding's red *R*—the closest thing the store had to a logo—in clever ways like drawer pulls and such.

"Just some ideas to give a designer I've found in Denver."

These sketches and plans were so specific Bo couldn't think why she'd need to hire an outside designer. Her vision for the store was as clear as day based on the papers in front of him. And it suited her: the entire project looked and felt like her. All the sophistication of her city life somehow slid back into her country mountain roots. It ought to have clashed, but it didn't. Actually, he found the whole concept pretty brilliant. She'd always had amazing ideas. He just never liked the idea she got in her head to leave him and all of Wander Canyon behind.

Bo let her walk him all the way through every design idea she had until he asked the hard question. "What's your budget for the project?"

Toni pursed her lips. She wore a touch of lipstick now. He liked that. "I don't want to ask Dad for money. I don't want him touching his retirement for this. So my budget is tight."

"Budgets are always tight around here. It's been a rough couple of years. We know how to do tight." He was making a point to use *we*, not *I*, as if this were a Car-San Construction decision. It wasn't, not really. This could never be anything but personal.

"I'm meeting with the bank tomorrow before Mari's shower, but near as I can tell, this is what I've got to work with." She pulled in a deep breath and pointed to a printout of a spreadsheet.

Bo hid his reaction. Calling the number at the bottom of that spreadsheet *barely doable* was a compliment. Truth be told, it was closer to unrealistic. Jake might have had another, less kind word for the low figure on that paper. Something like *nuts.*

Toni made the mistake—or the masterful tactic—of gazing at him with those mesmerizing green eyes. "I plan to be on this job as much as you, doing every bit of labor I can to keep costs down. I'll skimp in places when I absolutely have to, but I'm ready to reach for what I really want."

It happened just that quickly. Or maybe he just stopped lying to himself that he'd hadn't already decided to take the job. Oh, sure, it made a lot more sense to hightail it down to Florida where she couldn't hurt him again, but it was too late for that. Hearing what she wanted, the unsteadiness in her voice, the emotion of taking over Redding's—it all made it impossible to say no.

He couldn't bear the thought of any other contractor being involved. He was doing this job. It was a fitting last job to do in Wander Canyon before moving to Florida to start over. He'd gladly put in twenty-hour days to meet her schedule and maybe even absorb some of the costs on his own to help meet her budget.

He was doing this job. And doing it right.

Just this once, Bo allowed himself to invoke their history. "I'll do it. You'll get exactly what you want, Toni, at the cost you can pay. I owe you that much."

For a moment, he thought she was going to hug him. She certainly looked glad, even grateful. But after a moment's hesitation, she held out her hand for a professional handshake. And that told him everything about where the lines were drawn between them now.

Chapter Four

"That's the last of them." Toni set down the final heavy suitcase in her old bedroom only a week later. "I'm officially moved in. June 1 is the start of my new life back in Wander Canyon."

Dad hugged her tightly. "I guess that makes June my favorite month. I'm so glad to have you here." He looked at the trio of enormous suitcases now resting beside the handful of boxes Toni shipped a few days ago from New York. "I'm still amazed how fast you could make this happen. If it weren't for some help from Pauline and Hank, I'm not sure I could have had your room ready this fast."

Toni liked hearing how much other people in Wander, like Hank and Pauline Walker, the groom-to-be's father and stepmother, had pitched in to take care of Dad. But he was right; it had been whiplash fast—and startlingly easy—to extract herself from New York. What did it say that she was able to dismantle six years of her life in eight days? She'd found someone to sublet her apartment in forty-eight hours. "It was so easy I wonder if any of the past six years meant anything at all."

"It did. You had to test your wings out there in the big city, I suppose." Dad eased himself into the rocking chair in the corner of her room. "But I doubt it was that easy with Ms. Collins." He watched as Toni began transferring things from the suitcases to the bedroom closet.

She recalled the shock on Faye Collins's face when she told her boss she was leaving Hearth. "That *was* a bit tougher." She'd expected Faye to take it poorly, but the woman had seen it as a personal betrayal.

"After all I've done for you, you up and *abandon* me?" Faye had yelled, loud enough for the whole office to hear.

"I hoped she wouldn't hold me to the standard two weeks' notice," Toni told her father. "But she let me leave that day."

That wasn't the whole truth. Faye didn't *let* Toni leave that day—she'd *demanded* Toni clean out her desk within the hour. "You were already taking too much vacation time for this wedding business," Faye barked, throwing open the door to her office. "I don't want you working here another hour. Your precious vacation time starts this minute. Take it all and go."

"I know I hurt Faye by leaving so suddenly," Toni admitted to her father, not wanting to get into how ugly things had gotten between Faye and herself. She did feel bad about that. Faye had been a powerful—if extremely demanding—mentor. She'd always said how much she'd seen Toni as the daughter she'd never had. That was a balm of sorts after the loss of her own mother, and perhaps Toni had personalized their working relationship a bit more than was wise.

"Were things going well at Hearth?"

Toni sat down on the bed. "They were for a while. Everybody envied my job." Everybody outside Hearth, that is. Most people within the organization knew how difficult Faye was to work for and the kind of hours she expected of Toni. "People always said how fortunate I was to have someone as influential as Faye Collins take such a liking to me. At first, I thought so, too. I mean, who becomes Faye Collins's personal assistant right out of college like that? She's been on dozens of magazine covers and talk shows. I was kind of starstruck."

"What changed?"

Toni thought for a moment. "Me, I suppose. She was turning me into a version of herself, and I realized I didn't want to be that. I wanted to show New York what they were missing from the mountains. Turns out, nobody missed the mountains except me." She ran her hands along the stitches of the quilted bedspread her mother had made.

"Maybe I didn't change as much as I just remembered who I was and what I wanted." She looked at her father. "Faye was pretty heartbroken that what I wanted wasn't to be her protégée anymore," she ventured. "I do feel bad for blindsiding her like that."

Dad eased himself up off the rocker and came to sit beside her on the bed. "Sometimes the things we choose to do have a high cost. People get hurt. You do what you can to keep the hurt small and heal it, but that isn't always up to you."

Toni wondered if Dad was talking about Faye or Bo. The fact that his words could have applied to either left a sting in Toni's chest. Toni Redding, heartbreaker. That's not who she wanted to be.

She dared to ask, "Do you think I'm doing the right thing, Dad?"

Her father gave a soft smile. "I think you're doing a big thing. Whether or not it's right, well, that's only for you to answer. And I don't think you'll know for a spell." He took her hand and gave it a reassuring squeeze. "But I sure am glad you're giving it a try. And that you're here."

"And the store?" He'd seemed to come around to an enthusiasm for what she was doing, but her own doubts made her ask over and over.

"You're a Redding," he replied. "You're making a new Redding's. How could that not work out?"

A whole host of ways, Toni thought. "Bo and I start in the basement stock room tomorrow. I guess we'll find out."

Bo's stomach was in knots as he shouldered conduit and coils of wire off the back of his truck. First day on the job at Redding's. With Toni. He was trying to pretend this was a job like any other job. It wasn't working.

As he grabbed his toolbox, he caught Don Redding's wary gaze out the store window. The man hadn't spoken fifty words to him since the day Toni left, which was a clever feat in a town as small as Wander. They even went to the same church, and he'd managed to give Bo a wide berth for all those years. What did he think of this plan of Toni's? Or his role in it?

You hurt my baby, Don's furrowed brows seemed to say from the brightly lit window bay. He was momentarily glad Toni had gotten her stunning green eyes from her mother and not Don. When God was handing out eye color, He stuck around for a double shift at the Reddings'. It had always made him wonder why the trademark color for Redding's was red. Sure, Irene and Toni had red hair, and the color was built in to the name, but if you asked him, it was distracting jade-green eyes that made a Redding woman so hard to ignore. And impossible to forget.

He was ten minutes into this job, and already it was harder than he'd counted on. Some corner of his heart wanted to square off at Mr. Redding and shout, "Yeah, well, don't forget, your baby stomped on *my* heart!" He knew that was both stupid and useless. He and Toni were going to have to find a way past that if this job was ever going to work. All three of them would, in fact. He'd figured he would find a way to make peace with Toni, but he hadn't remembered he would have to make peace with Don, as well.

"You're here." Toni came up behind him with a pair of coffees and a large bag from the Wander Bakery. He wondered what was inside. She probably favored scones or some other high-brow pastry these days. "You're early."

The surprise in her voice pricked at him. *Yes, I'm grown-up and punctual now.* Truth was, early wasn't hard to manage when you barely slept. He was never anxious about jobs, but he'd been up all night worrying about this one. The construction aspects of this job were tricky enough, but the real challenge of this project had nothing to do with any blueprint.

Bo admitted no more than "Yeah," then added, "Much appreciated," as he lifted his coffee from the cardboard tray Toni carried.

She nodded toward the white paper bag as she pulled the shop door open. He noticed again that the door—in fact, lots of the storefront—was badly in need of a paint job. "Bear claws."

So she *did* remember his favorite. Bo wasn't sure what to read into that, if anything. Yvonne's bear claws were so good he decided not to care. A little sugar and a lot of caffeine would go a long way to helping ease things this morning.

Toni waved a bit too cheerfully at her dad as he stood in one aisle restocking some shelves. "We're starting in the basement," she called, barely slowing down in a beeline toward the cellar stairs.

They'd emailed several times and talked on the phone twice during her final days in New York, creating a flow chart of how the renovations would progress in order to keep half the store open the entire time. The conversations had been clumsy at first, but gradually they slid into a cautious partnership. It wasn't hard, given that she knew exactly what she wanted and he was determined to give it to her.

But face-to-face this morning, launching into the actual job, the awkwardness roared back. Toni in Wander was all real, all difficult and all permanent. Neither one of them would be able to easily run away from however this turned out. *But that won't matter much if I'm in Florida. Is that what this is showing me, Lord? That it's time for me to leave Wander?* Bo lobbed the question Heavenward as he followed Toni toward the door at the back of the store that led to the cellar.

They had agreed to start on the wiring in the basement because it made sense, but as Toni barreled down the cellar steps in front of him, he caught on to her real motivation. She was hiding.

Toni was in no hurry to navigate the maze of their first day while working together under her dad's glare. Good, because he wasn't, either. Hiding in the basement seemed as good a tactic as any. And the bear claws? He never could figure out how Toni kept such a figure when she could stress-eat better than anyone he'd known.

Bo took a fortifying sip of blissfully hot and strong coffee, slid the coils of wire off his shoulder onto the floor, and looked Toni straight in the eye.

Man, he was going to have to remember not to do that.

Instead, he inclined his head toward the store floor above them. "I thought you said Don was on board with all this."

She avoided his stare, digging into the bag instead. "He is."

Bo gestured again toward the staircase behind them. "Then what was all that about?"

She pulled out a bear claw and took a sizable bite. "All what?" It was entirely too cute how the flaky pastry garbled her words.

Toni may have been gone for six years, but he could still read her like a book. She talked vision and confidence, but she was as nervous as he'd ever seen her. He chose not to call her out on her false confidence, just raised a questioning eyebrow as he pulled his own bear claw from the bag.

"Dad's completely on board," she asserted.

"Then why are we hiding in the basement?" He wanted to see if she would admit the reason. It dropped like a stone in his gut when he realized it was very possible *he* was the reason. It wasn't that Don wasn't in favor of the renovation. He just wasn't sold on the *renovator.*

"It was your idea to start with electric."

It wasn't, but that wasn't anything worth clashing over. Not now when they had a thousand things ahead of them primed to start any number of arguments. Renovations were hard enough without the onslaught of history still tumbling between them.

Bo pulled a flashlight from his toolbox and began following the maze of wiring running across the cellar beams as he ate the bear claw. *Just get into it. Once you're doing actual work, it will get easier.* Besides, he didn't need any fatherly approval to make this job succeed.

He chose a diversionary tactic. "Is Mari ready for the big day?" Bo squinted at a pair of ancient connectors and pretended this was a job like the hundreds of others he'd done in his career. Jake usually handled electric, but he was only going to pull Jake into this when absolutely necessary.

Toni gave a small, tight laugh. "Of course she's not ready. Mari's a perfectionist, and she's going crazy trying to manage all the details."

Good, he'd gotten her talking. He handed Toni a roll of drawings Jake had sent over, being careful that their hands came nowhere near touching. "Is Wyatt helping?"

She managed another laugh at that. "Depends how you look at it. Is he calmer than her? Absolutely. But I think Wyatt would be happy passing out popcorn on the church lawn if he ended the day married to Mari." Toni cleared off a worktable and rolled out the drawings. "He's good for her. And she sure deserves to be happy after everything she's been through."

Bo wondered, had Toni had any serious relationships in New York? Given how fast she'd transplanted herself back here, he was going to guess no. But he certainly wasn't going to ask about her love life any time soon.

His examinations led him to the prehistoric fuse box, and he gave a low whistle. "Job one, right here." He pulled open the cover and began peering at the innards, glad to see a tangle that would keep him busy for most of the morning. The thing was a mess. Not unsafe, but certainly not up to code, and far too small for what Toni had planned for the store.

He poked around the fuses for a minute until a sharp "Okay, look," came from behind him.

He set down the flashlight and turned to face her.

She stood with her hands on her hips. "So this is a bit weird, I know."

A bit weird? Bo managed what he hoped looked like

a calm shrug. "Doesn't have to be." It became immediately apparent that wasn't the best response.

"But it does have to be professional. I just want to be clear that *this* is a business relationship. Clear margins."

You mean clear boundaries, Bo thought to himself. So she'd been worrying about this, too. The knowledge of her anxiety over how their mutual history could cloud things over only sharpened his radar. It was as if the air between them could either harden or soften, but it wouldn't be up to him. After all, she was the one who'd called him. She was in the driver's seat here, and the way her chin jutted out told him it had best stay that way.

"Absolutely," he agreed, because it seemed the safest thing to say.

Toni crossed her arms over her chest. "No cozy chats, no *remember when*s."

She wasn't drawing boundaries—she was throwing up twenty-foot walls. Given how much time together this job would take, would that even work? Maybe Peggy and Jake were right, and there was no hope for redeeming things with Toni. Maybe being this close to her really was going to end up as round two of the worst heart-stomping of his life.

"Look, I know you just want a friendly, effective, working partnership that gets the job done." The words tasted surprisingly sour to him. Still, he knew that's what she wanted to hear. Making peace with Toni meant starting from where she was. And where Toni was, right now, was behind a whole moat of anxious *stay-away*s.

"Yes, exactly." A bit of the rigidity left her.

"Okay, then, an effective start would be to move things off those shelves over there so we can get up into that ceiling." He made a mental note to use *we* whenever possible.

Because he had a different vision for the Redding's renovation. Insane as it was, Bo didn't want to just build a Toni a new store. Deep down, he was determined to build a new bridge. One that stretched over the years and crossed the distance between Toni and himself.

If he had to swim that moat to do it, he would. Or drown in the attempt.

Chapter Five

Toni lasted two hours down in that cellar storeroom before she climbed the stairs. She needed a dose of the sunshine that filled the store's main floor. It was cramped and run-down, but it wasn't especially stuffy down there. No, what drove her upstairs was how working beside Bo set up too much of a clash between wariness and nostalgia in her chest.

As she reached the top of the rickety old stairs, Toni brushed the dust from her jeans and her sleeves before pulling her work gloves off and tucking them in her back pocket. She craved a strong sense of accomplishment today, and so far it had felt like treading water.

Dad walked over from another aisle, where he'd been helping Jake Sanders's sister, Natalie, pick out coloring books with her young son. In this technological age, kids still liked to come to Redding's and pick out coloring books. She never wanted to jazz up Redding's so much that it lost that. "How's it going down there?"

"Fine, but I came upstairs to check my email." She

pulled her laptop from the counter drawer and set it out. "The first logo designs are coming in today. Want to tell me what you think?"

She was glad to see Dad's face brighten at being included. "Sure."

"Of course we're keeping the red *R*—I wouldn't dream of changing that," she reassured him. "We're just jazzing it up a bit."

Toni had always been a visual person. As such, the logo felt immensely important. It would set the tone for everything. It would be the first taste of her mark on the store. It had to be perfect. Everything had to be perfect.

Dad shook his head as he peered over her shoulder. "You kids and your technology." Her father had bravely mastered email and his cell phone, but the cash register at Redding's was as nondigital as they came—a beautiful old model that still made the classic *cha-ching* sound when anyone rung up a sale.

Toni held her breath as she clicked on the files attached to the email. "The designer is sending five ideas, and she'll refine the one I like best." Part of her winced inwardly at the use of *I*. "But I want your input, Dad. I want it to feel like a decision by both of us."

There was a moment of quiet as both of them viewed the collection of designs. Toni's response was as immediate and powerful as she'd hoped. One she could discard right away—it was too trendy. Three others were okay, but the one on the far right was close to perfect. It had a brushstroke look to it, but with a series of sweeping curves. Stylish and classic, comfortable and eye-catching. The full name swept across the screen in a dynamic way. Best of all, the designer had added a dash of yellow, managing to make the apostrophe before the *S* look like a twinkling star. Below the full name were a set of single-letter *R* logo/icons the designer had devised, each clever and distinct.

Something just short of glee filled her chest. "That one," she said, pointing to her choice before remembering to add, "Don't you think?"

Dad nodded his approval. "I like it. It looks—what did we say earlier? Newfangled?"

Even the designer had laughed when Toni gave her that word as a description. "Yeah, Dad. That's it."

"You're going to keep the red?" He looked touchingly surprised.

"Of course. I wouldn't dream of making the Redding's *R* anything but red. But you're okay with the touch of yellow?"

"Clever."

His approval felt huge. As though someone had just twisted a key in the lock that opened up her purpose. *Thank You for this, Lord*, she prayed as she hugged her father. She'd needed this moment to go well, and it had. That was enough blessing to combat all the friction of the last two hours.

As if on cue, the sound of Bo's boots on the store floor announced his ascent from the dusty depths. "I need some more wire from the truck." He must have caught the looks on their faces. "Everything okay up here?"

"New logo designs," Toni replied. "Want to see?"

Bo hesitated at first, then walked over. Together the

three of them peered at the sets of images. He considered them for a moment, and Toni felt herself putting far too much weight on which one he would favor. After all, it didn't matter which one Bo thought was best—this was her decision. This was going to be her store.

He pointed to the one she liked best. "That one. It looks like you." Then, as if he realized the nature of a comment like that, he stepped back and said, "I mean, it looks like what you've told me you want the store to be. But you should take it outside. You know, hold it up where the new sign would be."

There would be no more iconic use of Redding's new logo than on the store sign. Toni picked up the laptop and carried it out to the sidewalk. They had to cross the street to get the scale right—it was only a laptop screen, after all. When she held the full-screen image up to where the current Redding's sign stood peeling above the front door, they all leaned in and imagined the new sign in place of the old.

Perfect didn't do it justice. It was whatever was more perfect than perfect. It felt meant to be, if that made any sense. It was, quite literally, a sign from God. "I love it," she nearly sighed.

"Looks pretty spiffy, if I do say so myself," Dad said. After a second, he added, "I think your mom would have liked it, too."

With that comment, Toni felt as if the huge shift this represented in their lives fell into place.

After they finished in the basement, Toni and Bo spent an hour putting up plastic sheeting that split the sales floor in half so that one half of the store could stay open while the other half was under construction. Dad had spent the morning with a clerk shifting things around. It made things more complicated, but it honored Dad's wish not to close down completely.

What also made things more complicated—or at least annoying—was the barrage of emails Toni kept receiving from Faye.

I don't work for you anymore, Toni wanted to declare each time her phone pinged with a new text or email, each filled with sensible reasons why she should have stayed in New York. Faye was waging an unexpected campaign to get her back. Despite the woman's earlier anger, she now seemed bent on convincing Toni that going home to Wander Canyon had been a huge mistake.

It wasn't working. Mostly. The woman was ruthlessly persuasive, and Toni strove to tamp down her own doubts and fears as it was. *Being here is right, I know it is. Faye's just really skilled at pressing my buttons*, she kept telling herself.

Once the sheeting was up, she and Bo dug into the difficult task of the prying up the shop's old floor. Maybe back in the day green-and-white vinyl was the height of style, but now it just looked worn and hid the building's original wide plank floors.

Pulling the tile up proved a tedious nightmare. The stuff seemed to take delight in coming up in the smallest possible pieces, crumbling at the touch of a crowbar.

Bo started to make conversation to pass the time. "So tell me about the fancy New York job you just left."

He had no idea what he was asking, given the emails currently filling her in-box. "Executive assistant to... What was her name?"

"Faye Collins."

"Did you like your work?"

Toni shoved the crowbar under another piece of tile. "At first, I loved it. Working for Faye was hard, but exciting." Their conversation came in fits and spurts between shoves of their crowbars. "But..." Toni tried to think of a brief way to describe the all-consuming effect Faye had on people. "I ended up practically living at work. I slept on the office couch a few times. Faye is not the kind of person you say no to. Ever." Her smartphone was currently proof of that, wasn't it?

"But you did, didn't you? Well, it was more like goodbye."

She thought of the shattered look on Faye's face when she'd turned in her resignation. Loads of people had been fired from Hearth—most of them by Faye—but it seemed as if Toni had been the first to quit on the great Faye Collins. More than one colleague had told her she'd made a career-killing mistake. "She isn't taking it too well."

"I imagine you were a valuable employee to her."

"I think it went farther than that." It felt presumptuous to think about Faye in terms of being a mother figure, but they'd had that deep a relationship—at first. "She meant a lot to me. I like to think I meant a lot to her." Toni was surprised at how the words caught in her throat. "I wanted us to part on good terms, but I realize now that was just about impossible. You should see the emails and texts she's been sending me since I left."

Bo stopped working for a moment. "Wait… She's been contacting you?"

"A lot. She says she's worried about me. That no sane person would do this. That my life would be far better if I stayed in New York. That I'm just having some sort of emotional crisis that will pass." She stopped prying up a piece of tile and sat back on her heels. "She lays it out in excruciatingly logical detail."

Shaking his head, Bo replied, "So just delete them."

"I should."

"I take it this Faye person doesn't understand the concept of coming home to family."

"She actually calls me her family in one of her emails." Toni gave a dark laugh. "She feels abandoned, I suppose. But the real concept of family? Honestly, other than her long string of dramatic romances, I don't think Faye has a nonwork concept in her head."

Bo got an idea. A terrible, no-good, nonsense idea.

Even as he tried to dismiss it, he could feel the last shred of common sense and restraint slip through his fingers. "What if…" He looked at Toni carefully. "What if Faye thought you were having a dramatic romance of your own?"

Toni raised an eyebrow. "What?"

"What if you could convince Faye you came back to follow your heart? She couldn't give you any 'excruciatingly logical' reasons not to do that, could she?"

Toni shook her head. "No. But I've never talked

about having any kind of boyfriend here. I barely even talked about you."

Ouch, thought Bo. "Have you dated anyone seriously in New York?" Part of him really didn't want to know the answer to that question.

"Who has time to date when you're working for Faye Collins? I'm lucky I had time to sleep and eat. Besides, I don't think she'd believe I could take up with someone new that fast."

Don't do it, don't do it, don't do it... "What if it... wasn't someone new? What if it was someone old?"

"Huh?"

With a sensation that felt very much like throwing himself off a cliff, Bo continued. "What if we sent some photos back to make Faye believe you came back here to start things over with me? She couldn't compete with that."

She looked at him like he'd just gone totally mad. "That's crazy."

Yep, I just ruined everything. Bo looked at the floorboards, feeling as if his heart had just melted through them to puddle on the basement floor below. "Yeah, I know. Dumb idea. Wouldn't work. I never should have mentioned it."

An awkward silence gaped between them. Bo considered just leaving the building and calling the whole renovation project an utter failure until she said, "I don't know..."

All the air in the room disappeared. Bo was afraid to say anything, holding completely still.

She shrugged. "Faye's done her own share of crazy

things in the name of what she calls love. If nothing else, it might stop all these arguments she keeps throwing at me."

"We stage a few photos, you send them with some smitten-sounding emails and you get Faye off your back."

Toni looked like she was actually considering it. "She might actually back down for that. Honestly, I can't think of anything else."

Bo's heart had roared back up from the basement to thump wildly around in his chest. "I'd…um… I'd be okay helping you with this. I know it's crazy, but if it's the only thing that might work…" He was babbling, but she didn't seem to care. "We're already going to spend a lot of time together just to get this job done. It'd be easy."

This wouldn't actually work, would it? Surely he'd just proposed the worst idea in the whole world?

"Totally for show," Toni confirmed.

"Yep. Just one old friend helping out another old friend in a tight spot. Think of it as pest control."

She laughed, and he knew he'd won her over. It was insane. It probably spelled doom for his heart, but if he had no hope of getting Toni back for real, was it so awful to grab a chance to get Toni back just for show?

"Okay, then, get over here." Toni waved him over to sit up close next to her. "Might as well start now." Bo tried to keep his breath steady as he walked over and sat down next to her.

"You're really okay with this?" she said as she smoothed

down her hair and settled in close to him. Where were all her declared professional boundaries now?

Be careful, he told himself as he nodded. *This is dangerous.*

"Put your arm around me."

He gladly complied. Instantly he remembered the feeling of Toni in his arms, the perfection of how she fit against him. Bo swallowed hard and commanded his pulse to stay steady. Against his better judgment, he suggested, "Why don't you put your head on my shoulder like you used to?"

She did, and Bo had to look away for a moment, sure the pounding in his chest could be heard all the way to Denver. Toni angled her phone to capture them and snapped a few shots.

"These look great," she said. Was there a catch in her voice, or was he just imagining it? "Let's get a few more."

Oh, this was a *supremely* bad idea. Bo went along with her pose suggestions, the nearness of her driving him crazy. It wasn't hard at all to look like Toni had his heart. This was the farthest thing from professional distance. Peggy and Jake would be tossing him on a plane to Florida right now if they saw what he was doing. Only he didn't care.

Toni flipped through the photos with a fragile grin. "These look really...convincing. Who knew? That you were such a great actor, I mean?"

Yeah, Bo thought to himself, *that's it. I'm acting.* Nothing was less true in the world.

Surely it was just wishful thinking that convinced

him she looked flushed and unsettled. "I'm going to go send these. To my laptop, I mean. So I can write up a convincing email," she said, heading for the plastic sheeting that led into the other part of the store. "Can you get by without me for about twenty minutes?"

"No problem." Bo answered calmly despite the fact that every part of him was humming like a live wire. When Toni disappeared, Bo dashed to his truck and shut the door. He rolled up the window despite the heat of midday, picked up the clipboard so it would look like he was working on something and dialed Jake.

"I'm such an idiot," he groaned before Jake could get out a single word of greeting.

"Tell me something I don't already know." Jake laughed. "Exactly *why* are you an idiot—as if I couldn't guess."

Bo put his hand over his eyes. "I just came up with the worst idea in the world."

"Wouldn't be the first time."

"No, this is the worst. By miles. Toni and I just shot a bunch of pictures that make it look like we're back together to convince her old boss to leave her alone."

There was a stunned silence on the other end of the line. "I'm going to pretend like that makes any kind of sense. Because it doesn't. You *what*?"

Bo explained the situation, which only sounded even more absurd when he said it out loud.

"What were you thinking?" Jake asked. Well, actually he shouted it, but with good reason.

"I wasn't. It's only been half a day, and I can't think straight." *Those eyes of hers. They still tie me in knots.*

"Let's get you out of this. Head to Florida, and I'll cover for you. Parental emergency or some such thing. Peggy would back you up on this—you know she would."

"No." He wasn't going to lie to Toni.

Jake pushed out an exasperated breath. "So let me take over. I can push the Holmes's punch list off until tomorrow and be over there in ten minutes."

"I don't need a ringer." The consequences of his idiocy hit him. "Now I can't leave. At least not until the job is done. What if her boss doesn't believe her? What if she needs to send more photos?"

"That's not the real problem and you know it." Jake was tamping down his frustration—Bo could hear it in his voice. "The real problem is that you don't want to go to Florida because she's here in Wander. You want Toni back."

Bo took a breath to even try and counter that dangerous statement, but Jake pressed right on.

"Oh, I know you told me this whole project is to make it up to her, but it's not. Own up to it, man. You tell me different, but it's seeping out of your pores. You took this job for all the wrong reasons. You took it to win her back."

"Maybe." He hadn't taken this job for professional reasons. Just the opposite; there were a dozen professional reasons *not* to take this job. A wiser man would have listened to both Peggy and Jake, turned Toni down, and headed south for the winter as fast as he could pack his truck.

Toni had always made him crazy, and this time was

no different. This whole job was personal. It wasn't Toni who'd made an irrational career decision here—it was him.

"Maybe nothing." Jake sighed on the other end of the line. "Don't screw this up, Bo. I'm not happy you took the job, but you did take it. I think you should leave, but you won't. So do the work and get it over with. Don't turn this into some campaign to win back Toni. You don't need it, and I don't think she wants it."

Bo nearly winced. "I know you're right." That speech she'd given him about boundaries and margins couldn't have made her position any clearer. "She even told me so this morning." Still, he felt as if those moments with the photos seemed to tell him something completely different. Only he didn't trust himself not to be reading things into her actions that weren't there.

"Toni Redding is a customer, Bo," Jake insisted. "Nothing more."

Could Toni ever be *just a customer* to him? Today was just the first day—it would get easier. It would have to.

"I can do this," he told himself as much as Jake. "It's just way harder than I thought."

Chapter Six

The photos had evidently worked. During the rest of Thursday and all day Friday, no email from Faye arrived. Not even a text.

Problem solved. Or not. Something odd and unsettling had shifted between Toni and Bo while taking those selfies. *Oh no, you don't*, she told herself. *It's just an extreme solution to an extreme problem.*

From then on Toni had taken care to keep boundaries nice and clear between Bo and herself. They worked amiably but professionally as they struggled to pull up the rest of the flooring. Truth be told, the task was too exhausting to think of much else anyway. By the time the last tile had been yanked up late Friday afternoon, Toni had barely had thirty minutes to clean up before she and Dad went over to Wander Canyon Ranch, where Hank and Pauline Walker had invited her and Dad for a sweet little welcome-back supper. It was kind of them—they were always so kind to Dad—but she hadn't been good company. The truth was, rehabbing a store was hard work, and she was worn out.

Today, Toni ached everywhere. It might have been Saturday, but the fast-paced schedule she'd set meant today had to be spent ripping down the store's old, brittle wallpaper.

"I didn't think anything could be less fun than pulling up floor tile," Toni tried to joke as she yanked at a stubborn strip of the paper clinging to the wall in front of her. She grunted in frustration and wiped the hair from her forehead with the back of one dusty arm.

"Most fun ever," Bo joked. He looked just as wiped out as she was, and the day wasn't half over.

This was not fun. It was not energizing or purposeful or any of the things this drastic life change was supposed to be.

Toni wasn't averse to hard work—usually she loved it. But Mom would have called whatever overtook Toni this morning "a funk." Not that she would tell anyone how she was feeling.

No, taking over Redding's had to be full speed ahead. Full, energizing, purposeful speed ahead. Whenever Faye faced an obstacle, her battle cry was always "Be relentless!" *Okay, so be as relentless as Faye—just not as ruthless*, Toni told herself. But even taking the best of Faye's qualities while avoiding the worst hadn't saved her from this morning's ambush of wavering doubts. The overwhelming uncertainty felt like more than simple fatigue, and that unnerved her.

Wherever this funk came from, it would need to stay under wraps. She had to be Toni Redding, force of progress. Because Wander Canyon was watching—Wander Canyon was always watching. The determination to show the town what she could do steeled her spine.

With a grunt, she pulled harder on the paper—only to have a mere tiny bit shred off the wall in her hands. If she didn't know better, Toni thought the fussy old wallpaper was fighting her, digging its heels in to keep Redding's in the past.

It's just paper, she told herself as she went at the stuff with a razor-blade scraper for the hundredth time. *It doesn't have an opinion. It's ancient glue you're fighting, not some paper gumption.*

She laughed, finding *gumption* an old-fashioned word worthy of Dad and the midcentury wallpaper. You couldn't get farther from sleek Faye Collins and her chrome-and-steel corner office.

"That's better." Bo encouraged as he squeezed out the sponge he was using to wet down the old paper. "I like that more than the angry bear you've been sounding like all morning." He'd offered to be the one yanking the paper down, giving her the less taxing job of cutting slashes in the paper and soaking it to dissolve the glue, but she'd refused. For some reason she couldn't explain, she had to be the one pulling the paper down.

Toni stepped away from the wall. "It's fighting me. Hard."

Bo pulled a clean bandana from his pocket and dribbled water from his drinking bottle onto it. He squeezed it out over the bucket and offered the damp cloth to her. "It's wallpaper. Tearing down wallpaper is a form of torture outlawed by the Geneva convention in many parts of the world."

Toni put the cool cloth to her face, welcoming the sense of refreshment. She hadn't a shred of makeup on to ruin, so she pressed the cloth to her face with gratitude. She'd never been much for makeup—even though Faye was forever handing her cosmetics samples and had even bought her a spa day once—but she hadn't worn any at all since leaving New York. It struck her that had she been back in Manhattan, she would have hesitated to wet her face like this. Now, she did it with ease. It felt like one of a million tiny ways she was coming home.

"Wallpaper removal is not covered in the Geneva convention," she said as she wiped her neck. It felt like dust covered every square inch of her.

"Well, no." Bo shrugged. "But it oughta be, don't you think?"

Toni stared at the sinister wall—nowhere near as bare as her breakneck schedule demanded it be—and said, "Maybe."

"What's with you this morning?"

He could still read her easily. Maybe she could talk about some of her funk. It certainly was a safer subject than admitting those photos had knocked something loose in her locked-away feelings.

"This isn't..." it was a reach to find the words for it "...working the way I want."

She was grateful he didn't take her words as whining. "This is just the third day. Jobs like this are always harder and more complicated than you first think."

"I knew that. Or I thought I knew that. But it's more than just…complications. This isn't feeling the way I want." Could she safely make Bo understand it was the emotional struggle that was pulling the rug out from underneath her, not the work? "That makes no sense, I know."

"I think it makes perfect sense." Bo grabbed his water bottle and sat down on the floor with his back up against a wall still bedecked with faded blue flowers. A pattern Mom had chosen, Toni recalled with a pang. Mom showed up everywhere in the store, and that was as comforting as it was unsettling to change.

Bo pulled a second water bottle out of the cooler and motioned for her to sit, as well. She did, glad for the rest. "You're taking this massive step. Not only you, but your dad. You want it to feel the *good* kind of massive. You know, important, right, all that stuff. And instead it's just feeling overwhelming."

He'd managed to put it into words. He was always so good at that. "Yeah. How'd you know?"

"Every small-business person feels that way." Bo took a long drink and let his head fall back against the wall. "I knew launching Car-San was absolutely the right thing to do. I was sure I was ready. But for the first year, I'd get pummeled by these waves of 'what on earth do you think you're doing?' and 'you'd feel more certain if you were doing this right.'"

She nodded. Faye never seemed uncertain about anything. She felt a bit of the knot in her chest come undone at the thought that uncertainty wasn't necessarily a bad sign. Maybe she wasn't in way over her head the way it felt this morning.

"And I didn't have my dad watching every little step I take while I dismantled my parents' life's work and made it into something new."

Toni swallowed hard at the all-too-accurate description.

He gave her a long gaze. How did he manage to make mussed hair and face smudges look so charming? She was sure she looked a fright, but too much of her took notice of how handsome Bo still was. "It's a good thing you're doing," he encouraged. "You know that, right?"

"Most of the time, yeah."

Bo crossed one boot over the other. "That's all we can hope for."

Toni let her own head fall back against the wall, bringing up the vision of rustic barn wood paneling with gorgeous wrought iron shelving brackets she had planned for this wall. The fact that she could picture it so clearly made the fight to bring it into being that much more frustrating. *Why does it have to be so hard?*

"I want it to be so much more than just a renovation and reopening."

"So make it more."

Toni pulled her grimy knees up and hugged them to her chest. A month ago she'd never have been caught dead in the scuffed-up boots and grungy socks she wore today. She'd given away two-thirds of her New York clothes to a friend, knowing they'd look completely out of place here. There was something important about that. There had to be something truly important about all of this. “I don’t know how.”

“I know you. You’ll come up with something.”

They sat in silence for a minute, the box fan whirring in a desperate attempt to keep the sealed-off room from becoming a steam bath. She used the bandana to wipe her arms and hands.

“Could the reopening do something for the community somehow?” Bo asked. “You know, be bigger than just you and the store?”

Hearth did promotions like that all the time. Why hadn’t she thought of that? “Turn the opening into a charity event. A cause that Dad really loves. Maybe one that honors Mom, too.”

Together they looked at each other and said at the same time, “Summit.”

Summit Community Hospital was a cause near and dear to her family’s heart. When Mom’s heart troubles had started, SCH had taken care of her. SCH had been their source of help and care all the way until the end. A jar collecting change for SCH sat next to the Redding’s cash register to this day—and would forever, if Toni had any say.

Something new kindled inside Toni’s chest. “The opening could raise money for Summit. We could raffle off some items. I could work with Margaret Washington from the hospital volunteer board to put drawings from patients in the children’s wing inside all the picture frames. And not just that night—we could have a portion of all the sales for the week go to the hospital. Maybe for the whole month.”

Bo pointed at her. "That's the Toni I know."

Bo had guided her to something she'd only partly realized herself: Redding's had to be bigger than just her to work. It's why the store had stayed in business so long—it wasn't just about buying things, it was a community fixture. Her work at Hearth hadn't satisfied her because it was just commerce. Not that there was anything wrong with commerce, but she needed more.

The power of Bo's idea—and all the ideas that sprang to life beside it—was her best weapon against the wave of doubts.

Plus, Dad would absolutely love it. Mom would have, too. She welcomed the smile she felt cross her face and the burst of energy that came with it.

Bo gave a small laugh. "You want to run across the street and tell him right now, don't you?"

"I do," she admitted. In one of the first concrete signs of Dad's newfound freedom, Pastor Newton had managed to talk Dad into going out to lunch while a clerk watched the store counter. Normally, Dad never left the shop, even when other counter staff was there. "There should always be a Redding in Redding's," he and Mom had always said.

It warmed Toni's heart that with her arrival, Dad had felt able to accept the invitation to walk across the street to Gwen's. The sign out front called it the Wander Inn Dining Room, but since Gwen Rubins had run it for as long as Toni remembered, most of the locals just called it Gwen's.

He shrugged. "Then go. This can be a one-person job for half an hour."

"Nope," she said, rising up off the floor. "First I'm gonna show this wallpaper who's boss."

Bo's laugh grew loud and hearty as he heaved himself up off the floor, as well. "Now that's really the Toni I know."

That wallpaper didn't stand a chance.

It had been a long day. Bo was just about ready to call it quits late Saturday afternoon, but it wasn't going to happen. He could already tell what Toni was thinking as she stared up at the store's tin ceiling.

Since they'd tackled the floors and the walls, of course she was already plotting what to do about the ceiling. It was old and beautiful, but it only extended halfway back in the retail space the way she had reconfigured it. The new store didn't have—and didn't need—the large stockroom the old store had. They would be pushing that wall back in a matter of days. He thought it was a smart idea to make more retail space, but he could tell Toni was about to make a not-so-smart decision. Well, at least in his opinion—and he wasn't sure his opinion got to matter.

She stood there, neck craned up toward the detailed metal squares that made up the store's old-fashioned tin ceiling, planning. She'd want those burnished metal tiles to go all the way to the new back wall. Bo walked up and stood next to Toni, her thoughts so loud he could have guessed them blindfolded. "You can't," he said firmly.

"Can't what?"

"You can't have the tin ceiling go all the way back."

"Why not?"

"Because you're going to move the back wall, and there aren't enough tiles to cover a larger ceiling."

She brought her gaze down to look at him. "This can't be the only tin ceiling in Colorado. We can find more."

Bo sat back on one hip. Few things in life were more futile than explaining to Toni Redding why something wasn't possible. To her, everything was possible. It was her best and worst quality at the same time. "You won't find more. Not exactly like this, and not with the same patina if it comes from somewhere else."

She had the idea stuck in her head, he could see it. "So we'll mix. Find one that's close and alternate." She crossed her arms. "I'm not pulling it down, that's for sure." She made it sound as if the mere suggestion of pulling it down was an insult to the Redding's legacy.

Bo ran a hand across his chin. "Even if you could find some that complements this one, it'd cost a fortune. You can keep this one up, it just won't go all the way back."

She walked over to the wall where the tin ceiling currently stopped. "I can't have it stop here. That'll look ridiculous. It has to go all the way back. I'll find a way to get more."

He followed her, ignoring the small voice at the back of his brain yelling, "Don't get into it with her!" They were both tired and short-tempered. "It'll take you too long to find it and cost way too much. I'm cutting my labor costs to the bone here, but none of that will matter if you spend a fortune on nonessentials."

Wrong choice of words. "Nonessentials?" she repeated, frowning as if the word soured in her mouth. "So you're saying that the gorgeous tin ceiling that's been in Redding's since the day it opened is *nonessential*?"

He held up a hand in defense. "I didn't say that." When her frown deepened, he amended, "Or I didn't mean to say that."

"You said I couldn't have that ceiling go all the way back."

"What I was trying to say is that it's not smart to spend the money it would take to have that ceiling go all the way back."

She drew up her chin. "Isn't that *my* choice?"

A minor war was happening in Bo's head, with one part of him eager to please Toni and the other part of him knowing he would have to help her rein in her vision to succeed. There were customers who insisted on irrational choices in their renovations, ones who wouldn't hear his warnings about cost or time consequences. He'd let some of them have their way. Of course, they complained the loudest at the resulting price tag, and he'd swallowed the urge to say, "I told you so."

But Toni wasn't just any customer. She was going into debt to take over the store, and there were so many emotions tangled up in what she was doing. She wanted perfect and fast and frugal—things that rarely went hand in hand in the construction world without one other pesky word: *compromise*.

"I'm trying to help you."

"By telling me what to do?"

It was insane how easily they fell back into this old argument. Back when they were together, Toni would decide she wanted to do something and then launch into it no matter what. Sometimes that led to good things—like the fact that she was here and not still back in New York. Other times, she dug herself into holes—which she was in danger of doing now. "This is what I do for a living, Toni. I know what I'm talking about."

"Oh, and I don't? Hearth hired me right out of college. Faye hired me because of my great eye for decor. She was letting me do some of the buying before I left. I know what makes a space unique." She gave him that look. The one said, "I hate compromise." The one that was going to get her in trouble if she listened to her heart and not to her brain.

He walked over and picked up one of the tiles they had taken down to talk about how to protect it as they moved the back wall. It was a beautiful piece of work. He'd have fought her if she wanted to remove them, even though she'd probably get a load of money if she opted to sell them. "Look, I know you don't want to compromise—"

"I won't have to. We'll find the extra ceiling tiles."

"No, you won't." He was trying not to raise his voice, but it wasn't working. She could still get under his skin so fast.

"How do you know?"

"Because I already looked," he admitted, even though he'd planned not to tell her that. "The minute you talked about moving the wall, I knew that you'd want these to go all the way back. So I looked. Everywhere I know of—and I know a lot of places. The closest I came to a tile that would work would cost you too much, and that's even before we finish it to make the oxidization match. You can't afford it."

That silenced her. It should have felt satisfying to win the argument, but it didn't. Watching her have to compromise was like watching the light go out of her eyes. Disappointing Toni stung as much now as it always had. It's part of what had sent him into the tailspin when she left town—he'd never gotten over the notion that he'd disappointed her. Only there was no way not to disappoint her whether she went and he stayed behind or if he'd somehow been able to stop her from going. Toni had wanted what she wanted, and she'd wanted New York. More than she'd wanted him.

"You looked?" She sounded surprised.

"Of course I looked. Why wouldn't I look? I knew you'd want more of them."

The room felt big and empty in the silence that followed. Bo watched the disappointment round her shoulders and fought off the burn growing under his ribs. Toni slumped down against the wall, staring up at the ceiling as if it were some kind of enemy, snatching her dream out from underneath her.

It was just a ceiling. Not to her—not right at this moment—but it wasn't the battleground she was making it.

He went over and sat beside her, both of them staring up at the intricate tiles that would stop two-thirds of the way down the room when the wall was gone. He wanted badly to solve this for her. To be the hero of the ceiling tile—and everything else. Now who was thinking only with their heart and not their brain?

Several minutes went by. "I know you want it," he repeated.

"It's my favorite thing about the space." The way she said it, he knew her love for the store went so much deeper than even she had realized. It was her heritage, and she was striving to make it her legacy. Who would ever choose Florida over being a part of that?

Bo racked his brain for some way to give her what she wanted. "What if we spaced them out?"

She rolled her head to look at him, and his heart did a small flip. She was still the most beautiful—authentically, effortlessly beautiful—woman he'd ever known. "What?" The light started to come back to her eyes.

Bo grabbed a piece of drywall beside them and the pencil from his pocket. "Kind of a checkerboard. With… I don't know, maybe bead board or whitewashed barn wood and the lighting fixtures." He began sketching a pattern that integrated the tin tiles with other less expensive materials.

"We could make that go all the way to the back without buying more tiles."

Her use of the word *we* made him feel like a hero. That was worth an acre of tin tiles. They'd navigated their first squabble, and that was good.

But Bo sincerely doubted it would be their last.

Chapter Seven

Sunday was always a day away from the store, but this one truly offered a day of much-needed rest for Toni. It was also a special celebration—the first time she'd been home for her father's birthday in several years. She went to church with her father, after which Toni treated her dad to steaks at Gwen's.

"Eating lunch out two days in a row," Dad had mused, although she could see he was pleased. "I'm getting spoiled already."

"You deserve it, Dad." Toni's heart glowed in satisfaction at how their relationship was already deepening. Why had she waited so long to come home to this? How did she ever view the advantages of being Faye Collins's protégée as more important than being Don Redding's daughter?

The great meal was followed by a lazy afternoon that included a welcome nap. Now the day was drawing to a close around a fire in the backyard. Toni stared at the orange glow of the embers, awash in a sense of feeling settled.

A Sunday fire at sunset was a Redding family tradition and one of the most beautiful things about life in Wander Canyon. How many memories of roasting marshmallows and watching the stars come out filled her childhood? Even up on the roof of her New York apartment, the stars never laid out in the spectacular fashion Wander Canyon enjoyed most nights.

"I missed this more than I realized," she said to Dad as the two of them sat enjoying how dusk changed the colors of the sky.

"This yard is why we bought this house, you know. Your mother took one look at it and told me she could see nights like this in her mind." Dad paused for a moment. "I still feel her all over this house."

Toni couldn't tell if that was good or bad. "Is that okay?" she asked carefully.

"It is. This place is chock-full of good memories."

"It's also a lot of work, isn't it?" She'd noticed the house was showing as much wear as the store, maybe more. There were cracks in the driveway, and the kitchen sink leaked. One of the front steps' railings leaned over at a lazy angle, and the back fence had more than a few broken rails. "Did you ever think about moving? Downsizing?" She wanted him to feel free to do so if he ever chose.

Dad waved the thought away. "From this house? Never." He pulled in a deep breath of the night air. The air in Wander Canyon was a tonic all its own, crisp and clear and invigorating. The perfect backdrop for all those brilliant stars. "No," Dad went on. "Your mother and I had always planned to spend our retirement right here." She reached over and gave Toni's hand a squeeze. "I don't want to go anywhere else. Especially with you here."

"I'm glad," Toni said. It felt like a marvelous gift to give him years away from the strain of the store. "The store is so much work. I worried." He seemed to have aged too much since her last visit. Was he really managing fine on his own? Or just too proud to admit he wasn't?

"The store is a lot of work, yes. And it was easier when there were two of us, but I got by just fine. Will you manage okay on your own? Are you sure you don't need my help for a while?"

"You'll always be welcome at the store, Dad. And I'm sure I'll need your help now and then. But honestly, this is the perfect time for me to throw myself into it. And I'm not exactly alone. Bo's been a great help."

Dad gave her one of his looks. "I have to say, I was surprised you hired him. Lot of water under the bridge between you two."

"I know. And I won't say it hasn't been…weird at times. But I wanted everything to come from Wander, and we've worked out a couple of problems well together."

"Hmm," was all Dad said. That usually meant he was thinking about saying more. Still, it was his birthday. She didn't want to get into the thorny subject of whether or not hiring Bo was risky. She already knew it was.

As far as she was concerned, that risk had paid off

yesterday. Bo had been a good friend as well as a wise contractor, recognizing how her emotions were tied up in this project. He'd seen how her need for things to be perfect would skew her thinking. And he'd known her well enough to come up with an ideal solution. Dad wasn't wrong—this was a lot to take on alone—but Bo had proved himself a valuable partner yesterday. She still felt it had been the right choice to bring him onto the job.

But Dad was also smart to have reservations. Yesterday had also shown her she'd have to be careful. She'd have to keep those boundaries between her and Bo clear. With the selfies having done their job, Toni felt confident she could keep things squarely on a professional level. That hint of a pull she'd felt between them? That was as much of an illusion as the photos. Just the echo of a past love and nothing that should cloud her judgment or veer her soul off course. The last thing she needed right now was to muck up her future with feelings that should stay in the past.

Dad began snoring softly, pulling Toni from her thoughts. He seemed so much more tired lately. Toni reached over and shook his hand. "Wake up, Dad, you're sleeping." It was something Mom had said to Dad all the time when ne nodded off.

"Nonsense," Dad replied. "Just resting my eyes, that's all." There was something warm and wonderful that he'd given her the reply he'd always given Mom. Dad groaned as he labored to pull himself up from the deck chair. "I guess it's time for the old man to go to bed." He wheezed in a way that made Toni grab for his elbow, but he waved her away with a bothered grunt. "I'm fine, Toni. Just old. Old*er* today, I suppose. Besides, I want to be up bright and early to watch your newfangled awning being put in tomorrow."

My newfangled awning. Dad's words felt wonderful. Right after they'd selected the logo, Toni had ordered a spectacular new awning to show it off. Tomorrow it would be installed. It served as her unofficial announcement to all of Wander Canyon that Redding's was undergoing a transformation. The new awning was the first place the new Redding's logo would meet the world.

She doused the fire as Dad lumbered off toward the kitchen. She watched him open one of those big, multicompartment pill dispensers on the kitchen counter. It seemed to hold far too many tablets and capsules.

Dad was fifty-nine today. Next year would mark his sixtieth birthday. That was far too young to be elderly or frail, but he was definitely aging. Was he ailing? Or just ready for the retirement she was about to give him?

Monday couldn't come fast enough. Toni knew she was making too much of a simple awning installation, but it felt so incredibly important. As the truck arrived, she felt her future arriving with it.

Toni and her father sat on one of the rough-hewn log benches across the street from the store for the best view to watch the process. The ornate bench in front of Redding's—red wood with wrought iron sides—had always stood out from the log ones that dotted Main Street up and down the center of town. Of course, Bo had moved the Redding's bench out of the way for this morning's installation. Before taking its place back in front of Redding's big display window, the bench would be painted by a group of town kids from the Summit Community Hospital junior volunteer corps in a promotional event later this week.

The storefront looked empty without the bench, especially with only a New Redding's Coming Soon sign in the front window. Bo walked across the street to stand by them just as the installation crew started pulling the old awning down. She appreciated that he was supportive, but she also was grateful he sensed that the power of this moment belonged to Toni and her father.

Toni took her dad's hand as the crew started dismantling the old awning. Did Dad feel the moment tug on his heart the way it did on hers? The change of awning had become a symbol for everything that was happening. The physical manifestation of the transformation happening in their lives and the store.

"Your mother chose that awning," Dad said, his voice thick with emotion. "It's been up since the day we opened." He squeezed Toni's hand. "We were just a couple of young, hopeful newlyweds back then."

"You two were great partners, Don," Bo offered.

"The best," Toni added. She couldn't think of finer equal life or business partners than her mother and father. *I want that*, Toni thought as she looked from her father to the storefront. *I want to believe that a partnership like they had is in my future.* Today felt like a big step toward that future, even though the leap felt scary and enormous.

The awning was such a fixture of the store that she'd never really paid much attention to it. Looking at it now, she could see how old it really was. Weary-looking. The once-bright colors had long since faded, and decades of wind and weather had tattered the fabric at the edges. The letters were cracked and curled like old leaves.

The three of them fell silent as the crew pried the old awning off its brackets. It pulled away from the building with an eerie metallic groan. Some part of Toni's heart wished it hadn't collapsed into such brittle pieces as it hit the ground. She had the urge to rush across the street and gather it up, needing to lay it to rest rather than let it be piled into the truck as scrap.

She didn't. It was just an awning. Just old canvas and rusty piping. What made Redding's Redding's was sitting on this bench, not on that sidewalk.

The quiet lasted far too long as the crew continued to work. No one mentioned how bland and empty the storefront looked without its awning.

And then the crew went back into the truck and pulled out the most beautiful awning in the whole world. Toni actually thought she might cry when the protective plastic was ripped off and the new awning was welcomed into the world.

Perfect. It was the only word she could find. Even though she'd seen the design drawings, in real life it was exactly the way she'd hoped. Everyone watched as the crew hoisted it up and fastened it to its new brackets above the window. Was it silly to say the building felt whole again with the new awning in place? Ed from the barbershop next door and a few other people even came out from their stores up and down the block to watch. Toni welcomed the affirmation of the small crowd that gathered.

They seemed to like it. She loved it—every single thing about it. The fabric was a dove gray, light enough to glow when lit, but dark enough not to ever look dirty no matter what the Colorado weather threw at it. The tail of the spectacularly big swirly *R* swept a graceful arc under the rest of the red letters. A bright yellow half star, half apostrophe winked from atop the name. Toni's heart positively hummed at the sight.

Still, she was also astonishingly nervous. Toni kept stealing glances at Dad on the bench beside her. He'd seen the drawings and expressed his approval, but this was the real deal. This was the new Redding's bursting into existence.

It seemed ages before Dad nodded and said, "I like it." He slipped his arm around Toni. "Definitely newfangled."

He didn't look well this morning. She'd even tried to convince him to stay home, despite knowing that was a futile pursuit. No way was Dad ever going to miss this.

"I'm perfectly capable of getting out of the car to sit on a bench on the sidewalk and stare at a window," he'd groused when she'd offered to just drive him by the shop once the new awning was up.

"Did Toni tell you it lights up?" Bo asked, pulling her back to the present.

"She did." Toni didn't like the way he wheezed with the word.

To her, the lighting would be the best part. She'd

worked hard to hit just the right balance. The lighting in this awning wouldn't be so bright that it would look like some out-of-place neon sign on Main Street in little Wander. No, it was just enough to glow a silvery welcome when the sun went down. Oh, she'd still keep the tradition of turning on the sconce lights on either side of the window when the shop closed up for the night, but now the awning would add its silvery-red glow all night long. Toni liked to think the yellow apostrophe would feel like a star in the night sky. She wanted the awning to send the message *we'll always be here for you.*

"Well, let's go see the thing light up," Dad said, grunting his way to standing. Without any more ceremony than that, he started back across the street. "How do you switch the thing on?"

He nearly missed the curb, and Toni dashed to his side to catch him as he toppled a bit. "It will be on a light-sensing timer, Dad. We won't have to switch it on."

"Well, doesn't that sound newfangled?" He grabbed a handkerchief out of his pocket and wiped his forehead. Had he been sweating this whole time? It was a bright day but not especially warm out.

"Sure, Dad. Newfangled." Toni didn't think timed lights were especially high-tech, but she took her father's elbow and Bo came to stand on Dad's other side. The three of them began to make their way across the street.

Dad was awfully slow. "Hmm," he grunted. He slowed his steps and stopped walking halfway across the street even though traffic was coming in both directions. The car in the lane in front of them slowed down to let them continue their laborious crossing. It made Toni think of how that would never, ever happen in Manhattan. A fast pace to cross busy streets was an essential New York survival skill.

As she reached back to urge him along, Toni caught site of the focus leaving her father's eyes. He face looked too pale. He was breathing in a way that didn't sound right.

"Dad, are you— Dad!"

"Don!" Bo called.

In some awful version of slow motion, Toni watched her father wobble a bit, grunt again and then begin tipping forward toward her.

Chapter Eight

"Dad!" Toni cried out as she grabbed at her father's falling form. But he was a big man, and she wasn't ready to catch the full weight of him as he slumped against her. He was sweating, but his skin was unnervingly clammy to her touch. Everything about him looked and felt wrong. Bo was beside her in an instant as Dad went limp in her arms and three of them ended up tumbled onto the yellow stripe down the middle of the road.

Toni scrambled to her knees as Bo tried to ease Dad onto his back. Her father's eyes were eerily glassy and unfocused before they fluttered closed. She grabbed one hand and put to other to his chest. The hand was limp—far too lifeless—but she was grateful to feel his chest rise and fall with struggled breaths. She reached to his neck. She had some idea what a healthy pulse felt like, and this didn't feel healthy at all.

"Dad— Can you hear me, Dad?" Toni touched her father's cheek and shook his shoulder gently.

Toni's brain began collecting a strange assortment

of details. The heat of the asphalt on her knees, the sun beating on the back of her neck, the way Dad's gray eyelashes looked against his pasty skin.

Bo was already on his phone. "I've called 911," he said. "They'll be here any minute."

"I knew there was something wrong," Toni whispered. "He hasn't looked right lately." Dread wrapped steel bands around her chest. "Don't leave me, Dad. You can't leave me."

The desperate plea seemed to somehow reach her father, for his eyes opened. "Irene?" he gasped out her mother's name, making Toni's heart lurch.

He sounded awful, but he sounded alive. Dad was sick. Sicker than he let on. She'd suspected it. And she'd been cowardly enough to ignore it because it was such a scary thing to consider.

"No, Dad, it's me, Toni." *I can't lose him*, Toni prayed as she gripped her father's hand. *Not now, Lord. Please.*

"Hang on, Don," came Bo's voice. "They're on their way."

Cars driving the other direction stopped, and a small crowd began to gather around the scene. Toni saw their shadows on the street surface, heard their voices and even some of their prayers, but she would not take her eyes off her father. If her gaze could hold him to this world, she'd try. She couldn't bear the thought of him slipping away if she turned her glance away for even a second. It was probably only minutes, but it seemed like an eternity until a few short blasts of sirens parted the crowd and an ambulance pulled up next to them.

"They're here, Don," Bo said. "Okay, everybody, give them room."

"They're here," Toni repeated, the panic in her voice cutting through her chest like a storm of knives. "Hang on, Dad, the paramedics are here. You'll be fine soon."

A flurry of technical commotion—equipment and gloved hands and radio noises—surrounded Dad. Bo tugged her slightly back, but stepping away to let them assess Dad felt like the groaning rip of the awning being pulled off the building. It made her physically ill to be even an inch farther away from him.

The paramedics were quick, but they were calm. No one was making moves like they would start CPR or get out a defibrillator. Was that good? Was it a stroke? His heart? Something else? They weren't scrambling—did that mean Dad was going to be okay?

One of the paramedics—someone she vaguely remembered from high school—began relaying a slew of medical terms over a radio. The words came at her like a hailstorm; Toni could hear them hit the window of her brain, but she couldn't see through the glass to know what they meant. A few single words like *cardiac* and *stabilize* made their way through, but she couldn't string them together to make any sort of sense.

Bo's arm came around her. "I'll drive you to the medical center behind the ambulance." He had to repeat it twice until the words clarified enough to make sense. Toni couldn't seem to make her legs move.

"Come on," Bo insisted.

Dad made the most horrible pained gasp as they raised the gurney. Toni lunged to try to stay beside him, but the familiar paramedic held out a gentle hand. "You can't, Toni. We've got him. It's going to be okay. Just let Bo drive you."

With his calm pronouncement, the man and his partner slid the gurney into the ambulance. With a peculiar oddness, Toni noticed the clatter of the gurney's folding legs. She couldn't decide if it sounded like the collapse of the old awning or the snapping into place of the new one.

Either way, it still looked as if Dad was being swallowed up by some terrible square red whale.

A split-second spike of fear seized her limbs—would she ever see Dad again? She was openly crying now. Bo asked her something as he eased her shaking body into the passenger seat of his truck.

"What?" The words were just hail again, hitting the glass of her panicked brain.

"Does anyone else have a key to the store?" he asked slowly as the truck rumbled to life.

"You," she managed. "And Ed from next door."

Bo rolled down his window as he pulled the truck out of its parking place. "Ed, can you lock up the store?"

"Absolutely!" came Ed's voice as he stood outside his barbershop next door to Redding's. "You take care now! I'll call the church prayer chain."

Yet another tiny little human kindness that would never happen in New York. *I wouldn't be here now if I was in New York.* Why hadn't she noticed how poorly Dad was feeling earlier? *I should have noticed,* she thought to herself. The burning guilt that she should have seen the clues seared her chest. The store was too much for him without Mom, and had been for a while. *Don't let it be too late*, she prayed. She'd been so happy to see the way Dad's eyes lit up in pleasure at the new awning. Now all she could see was the emptiness in those same eyes as he'd slumped down against her. *I'm not ready for him to go. Don't make me say goodbye. Not now. Not when we should have so many good years left.*

Feeling more tears slip down her cheek, Toni reached for Bo's hand and squeezed it tight.

"Hang on," he said, squeezing it right back. "I'm here."

Wander Canyon was a small town, but it loomed as wide as an ocean as Bo tried to weave through the streets to the urgent care center on the east side of town. He offered a few heartfelt words of comfort to Toni, but it looked as if nothing was getting through the fog of fear that surrounded her. *Why today, Lord?* Bo questioned. *Toni told me it was his birthday just yesterday.*

He'd called his own father just to check in, but that wasn't the same thing as being there in Florida with them, was it? They asked him when he would be coming down, and he couldn't bring himself to name a date. *We've got time*, he told himself, but did they? Couldn't some episode snatch Dad or Mom from him just as easily as Don had gone down today?

Bo swung the truck into the urgent care center parking lot, and together he and Toni took the entrance steps two at a time. A few construction mishaps had familiarized him with the waiting room, so he knew to lead her left.

Doc Webster, the physician who seemed to take care of everyone in Wander Canyon, was standing in the waiting room to greet them.

"Is Dad gonna be okay?" Toni asked as she dashed across the room. It wasn't hard to see the fear that widened her eyes. After all, she'd come home to be near her dad, not to face the threat of shortened time with him.

"We don't know yet," Webster said. "Dr. Gillen is in with him now, and they're running tests."

"Who's Dr. Gillen?" Toni asked in a shaky voice.

"He's your father's cardiologist. Didn't you know?"

"No!" Toni nearly shouted. "Dad never said anything about a cardiologist."

"Gillen is very good. Let me go in there and see when they'll let you see him, okay?" He gave Bo a "keep her calm" look and headed back through the double doors of the treatment bays.

Bo tried to steer Toni toward a seat in the waiting area as he grappled for the right thing to say. This comfort stuff had never been his strong suit. "That's good. A specialist who knows his history is good, right?"

Toni pulled away from him and wrung her hands. He could see what was happening—it was written all over her face. The guilt over not coming back to Wander and taking the store off Don's hands earlier had begun to take hold. She was in for a rough ride if she let that guilt press her into bigger and faster plans for the store—which would be just like her to do. Or it would paralyze her into stopping everything and leaving Redding's closed, which would help no one, least of all her. If this was just some episode and Don was going to be okay, Toni probably ought to keep going, but right now it would be a battle to keep her at an reasonable speed. *I can help her with that. Let me, Lord*, he prayed.

What would Pastor Newton say? Surely he was on his way, but Bo was the only one here now. Rather than come up with words, he simply pulled Toni into his arms and held her tight. He liked the way her head found the perfect spot on his chest to rest, the way she felt in his arms. It was both excruciating and wonderful. And he was so grateful to be here for her.

She clung to him for an unguarded moment, all those carefully drawn boundaries dissolved by the crisis. But all too soon, Bo felt her pull back as Doc Webster returned through the doors.

"You can see your father in a minute or two. Dr. Gillen's going to have him moved over to the hospital to do some tests. It doesn't seem to be a heart attack, just his A-fib acting up more than usual," Webster said.

Toni's words echoed Bo's own thoughts. "His heart? What's A-fib?"

"Atrial fibrillation. He's been having episodes for about six months. You didn't know?"

Bo remembered Don's name coming up on the church announcements. It made him wonder just how small that episode really was. If Don hadn't told Toni—which clearly he hadn't—she wasn't happy about it. He couldn't blame her. If she really had been considering moving back for several months, it would only make matters worse to know what she'd missed by waiting.

"I didn't know anything about it. Why didn't he tell me?" Toni demanded.

"You'll have to ask him that." The doctor put a gentle hand on Toni's arm. "I'm sure he just didn't want to worry you. A-fib can be well controlled—"

Toni yanked her arm away. "I should have come home months ago. That's what I should have done."

"Let's all try and stay calm here."

Toni started shaking her head over and over, her eyes welling up. "He should have told me. He should have known he could tell me. I would have been here. I would have taken over *so much earlier*."

"I know you're upset," Doc Webster said.

Bo pulled the bandana from his pocket again. He kept handing it to her so she could wipe her tears, and she kept giving it back to him. "Let's all sit down for a minute," he said, trying to sound comforting. "Let's hear what else the doc has to say before we get worked up."

She looked far from convinced, but at least she sat down. Bo was just thinking maybe things were going to settle down when his phone started buzzing, showing a local number. Had something gone wrong after they left?

"I'm going to take this call," he said, stepping a few feet away. If something was wrong at the store, he wasn't going to add it to Toni's worries.

"Bo, it's Ed. Everything okay over there?"

He stole a look back over to Toni and Doc Webster. "A bit soon to say. Doc Webster says they're going to take Don over to Summit to run a few tests."

"I suppose that's good news."

"I hope so. What's up?"

"Well, I've got a fancy lady here who came into the store as I was locking up. She says she's looking for Toni."

"Now's not a good time for her to be taking calls."

"That's what I said, but this lady says she needs to talk to Toni right away."

She just rushed her dad to the hospital and some vendor needed to talk to Toni right away? "Yeah, well, why don't you get her name and number and I'll pass it along."

Bo heard some conversation, and then Ed came back on the line. "She's from New York. Says her name is Faye Collins."

Chapter Nine

Bo couldn't have heard right. "Who?"

"Faye Collins," Ed repeated. "Says she's a good friend of Toni's. Maybe I should send her over? Toni will need a ride home, won't she?"

Faye Collins was here? In Wander Canyon? *Now?*

Bo stepped a few more feet away from Toni and Doc. Maybe it wasn't his job to decide, but he didn't think right now was a great time for Toni's insistent old boss to show up unannounced. Toni didn't work for her anymore. Then again, hadn't Toni said Faye didn't know how to take no for an answer?

Bo pinched the bridge of his nose, scrambling for the right way to handle this new wrinkle. "I'm not so sure now's the best time. Toni is dealing with a lot of stuff."

"But Don's gonna be okay?"

"I think so, but things could still get complicated."

He couldn't *not* tell her, despite how sorely tempted he was to keep the information to himself. "I'll tell her," he answered Ed, "and you let Ms. Collins know

Toni will get in touch with her when she can." After a moment's thought, he added, "But maybe hint that it won't be soon, okay?" He had to buy Toni a shred of time. "And certainly don't send her here. I can bring Toni back when she's ready." He would absolutely be the one to bring Toni home. The stack of estimates on his desk would just have to wait until things calmed down.

Bo clicked off the call and gulped. Faye Collins was here. In Wander Canyon. The woman's actions set off an alarm in his gut. It didn't take a genius to figure out why: Faye was about to launch an all-out attempt to lure Toni back to her old job.

On today's list of unhappy surprises, Faye Collins had just shot to the top.

Toni walked out to the front steps of Summit Community Hospital and told herself to take deep breaths of the fresh air. Why did hospitals always smell like... hospitals? Doc Webster and Dr. Gillen had talked her through the upcoming tests. Then Doc told Bo to go get Toni some lunch so that Dad could nap.

In the time that it had taken to transport Dad from the urgent care center to the hospital, Toni had arranged for her aunt Roseanne to come in from Colorado Springs to help out for a few days. Bo had lent a hand by contacting two of the store clerks to pull extra shifts to cover the store. Pauline Walker had launched the church benevolent society into action so that a week's worth of food was already set up to be delivered to the house. Some days Wander's watching also meant the community could kick into gear in a flash to help out one of its own.

Toni felt like she needed a nap herself. They'd run one test on her father and were going to keep him two days to run a few more—and perhaps put in a pacemaker. Dr. Gillen made it sound like a routine procedure, but it didn't sit that way with Toni. The idea of Dad needing something so drastic-sounding as a pacemaker left Toni in a fog of worry. The gift of all those store-free retirement years felt as if it was slipping though her fingers.

She'd waited too long. She'd ignored too much. She'd been too selfish with her own goals to tend to her father's well-being.

Bo had not left her side while she navigated through the deluge of doctors, tests and plans. He was being a good friend, and she was certainly thankful for that.

But there were hints of more. The moment he'd held her in his arms back at the urgent care center had stunned her. The staged selfies had been an echo of who'd they'd been before, but his embrace this morning felt like a deep dive into that history. All the years and distance evaporated, leaving her in a place that felt both familiar and unsafe. It had taken an awful lot to pull herself back out of whatever that moment was, and that frightened her as much as Dad's episode.

Toni took in another deep breath, letting the silence replace the sounds of all those beeping monitors and murmuring doctors and nurses. She looked at her watch. It seemed as if they'd hoisted the new Redding's awning five weeks ago instead of five hours. Unsteady in the storm of chaos, Toni sank down on the warmth of the concrete steps and hoped her churning stomach could welcome whatever it was that Bo was able to scrounge up from the hospital cafeteria.

A shadow passed over her, and she looked up to see Bo standing there with an armful of food. “You can do healthy—turkey breast on whole wheat and fruit—or you can opt for the comfort food special.” He held up a bag of cheese curls and a diet soda. Evidently he remembered her snack favorites. “I couldn’t decide which you needed more.”

She squinted up at him, then pointed to choose the snack bag and can of soda. “What were you going to eat?”

He pulled a candy bar from his shirt pocket. “This and whatever you didn’t want.” He’d always had a sweet tooth, unlike her craving for salty foods. Setting the sandwich down, Bo unwrapped the candy bar and broke off a square. “He’s gonna be okay. You know that, don’t you?”

“But a pacemaker?” She still couldn’t say the words calmly.

“Norma Binton has one of those. It didn’t help. She’s just as mean as ever.”

Old Biddy Binton. Mari had mentioned something about her having a field day with her and Wyatt’s unconventional courtship. She knew Bo meant it as a joke, but she had no laugh in her.

“So,” Bo said with a nervous exhale, “now that we have a moment, I…um… I’ve got some news.”

Toni opened the soda can. “If the zoning board has some issue with the awning, now’s not the time.”

"No, the awning's fine. This is a bit more…unexpected."

"What?"

"Someone's here to see you." Bo had the oddest tone of voice when he said it.

She ate a handful of cheese curls. They were deliciously awful. "I don't think Dad's ready for visitors just yet."

"No, to see *you*. Here in Wander."

She didn't have the mental capacity to solve verbal puzzles at the moment. "Huh?"

Bo pushed out a breath and turned to face her. "Faye is here."

She couldn't have heard him right. "What?"

"Your old boss, Faye Collins? She's here. She showed up at the store just after we left."

Today slid from chaos to absolute absurdity. "Faye is here? In Wander?"

"She walked into Ed's barbershop looking for someone to tell her why the store wasn't open."

Toni could barely keep from spilling the drink. "She's here? She can't be here."

"She is." There was something comforting about how outrageous Bo found it—it was outrageous. Ridiculous. Beyond even someone like Faye.

Toni felt her temper boil up. "I don't want her here. I don't work for her anymore. She has no business being here. Tell her to go back home." She let her head fall onto her knee. "Faye can't be here."

"Faye is here. And she wants to see you. I told Ed to

hold her off from coming over here, but based on what you've told me, I don't think that will work for long."

"No," she moaned, with her head still down. "It won't." She picked her head up to look at Bo. "Why is she here?"

"To convince you to come back, I suppose." Bo sounded miffed.

This could not be happening. "I'm not going back. I'm not some prize pet who ran away from home."

"I know that, and you know that, but Ed told me she asked where the best hotel in town was." Bo didn't bother breaking off a piece of chocolate this time, just took a huge bite out of the bar. "Seems your boss has plans to stick around."

"*Former* boss," she corrected, getting truly annoyed now. "As in *not anymore*."

"I don't think she got the message."

If she'd really thought about it, she probably would have realized Faye might do something like this. Faye just couldn't comprehend that anyone would refuse her anything. She probably felt she was on a mission of mercy, here to help her misguided protégée wise up and repair the error of her quitting.

Toni decided she wasn't going to stand for such nonsense. Faye absolutely could not show up here at the hospital. Faye was going to turn around and go home. As fast as possible. "Can I borrow your cell phone? My handbag is still at the store."

Without a word, Bo unlocked his phone and handed it to Toni. She thought about calling Faye but decided against it. Aunt Roseanne would be here in about a half an hour, and this had to be handled face-to-face. She'd make sure Faye saw the determination in her eyes. Toni punched in Faye's cell number and began typing.

It's Toni. Meet me at the store in twenty minutes. Then in a fit of annoyance, she added, Don't unpack.

The reply came back instantly. Already did. Been trying to call you. Sorry about your dad. I'll be there.

She looked at Bo. "I need you to drive me to the store once Aunt Roseanne gets here."

It looked like the last thing he wanted to do. "You don't need to do this. I'll be glad to chase her off for you."

"Thanks, but I highly doubt she'll listen to you. I've got to swing by the house and pick up some stuff for Dad anyway. He's got that second test in an hour, so I'd just be sitting in the room waiting for him, and Aunt Roseanne can do that." Toni stood up. "And I need to take care of this now. I don't want Faye in this town for a single night."

Bo stood up, as well. "I'm not leaving you alone with her."

"I'm a big girl, Bo. I can handle Faye."

"I didn't say I'd help. I've no doubt you can tell her off just fine on your own. I'm just not leaving you alone with her. If you meet her at the store, I'll be there."

She didn't have time to argue this. "Not in the same room."

"Fine."

"Fine." Before she turned toward the hospital doors, she picked the bag and can back up. Had she thanked him for all his kindness today? She could no longer think straight with all the chaos surrounding her. "Thanks for these."

As she walked up the steps, Bo called behind her. "Faye sounds like a dragon lady, by the way."

Toni thought about the joke around the office that Faye had hatched from a dragon egg. She'd scrambled a hard path to the top and had taught Toni a lot about fighting for what you want. The trouble with Faye was that she just didn't know when to stop fighting.

"Well," Toni replied, "I've learned a thing or two about slaying dragons."

As they pulled up to the parking spaces in front of Redding's, Bo felt like he could have picked Faye out of a crowd if there were a hundred people lining the sidewalk. The well-dressed woman standing under the Redding's awning looked *exactly* as Bo had imagined her—a pair of ridiculously high heels, sleek hair, power clothes, fierce sunglasses, too-red lipstick. Even the way she carried her enormous handbag broadcast the air of a woman who always got her way. She lowered her sunglasses as if it was a peculiar sight to see Toni getting out of a pickup truck.

Bo gave a small grunt—maybe more like a snort—as he cut off the truck's ignition and handed his keys to Toni. She'd given him a key to Redding's, and her store keys were still inside, where she'd left her purse in the rush to get Don into the ambulance.

Her face was unreadable as she wrapped her fingers around the leather *B* that still was his key chain. She'd given the fob to him as a graduation present. Did she remember? Did she notice?

"You keep out of this," Toni said like a scolding mother.

"Yes, ma'am," Bo muttered as he climbed out of the truck. *But I don't want to. I'd love to tell this lady what I think of her uninvited visit.* He pretended to fish something out of the truck bed so he could let Toni reach Faye first.

Faye hugged her, but Toni pulled away quickly and used the key on his ring to open up the shop. He kept a reluctant distance as he grabbed his toolbox and followed the two women into the store. Toni was strong. She could handle herself, even with this dragon lady, even after the morning she'd had.

Toni and Faye stood in the cluttered space that was the still-functioning store. Only Faye wasn't looking at the space, she was sizing up Bo. The woman's gaze quickly cataloged the paint smears on Bo's shirt, the dust all over his pants, the hole in his shoe and the rip down one sleeve—as if she'd never seen work clothes before. "You're him."

She said it as if Bo had stolen something of hers. He chose to take that as a good sign, evidence that his idea of the staged photos had worked. He simply nodded.

All three of them stood for a moment, not talking. Faye was clearly waiting for Bo to make himself scarce.

"Yeah, well, I'll be just over here if you need me." Bo tried to make it sound like as much of a warning to Faye as it was a promise to Toni. He didn't trust this woman. A woman who flew halfway across the country could be prepared to promise Toni just about anything.

Including whatever would lure her back.

Not happening, even though it wasn't anything close to his call.

"I'm sure we'll be fine," Toni said as Bo pushed the curtain of plastic sheeting aside. He wasn't even out of the room before Toni launched into it. "Why are you here, Faye?"

It pleased Bo that her question sounded more like an accusation. Bo stood just on the other side of the sheeting—technically out of the room, but where Toni could see him and know he heard everything being said.

"Toni..." Faye began in a maternal tone, extending a hand toward Toni's cheek.

Toni pulled away and tossed the key chain onto the counter. "I mean it, Faye, why on earth are you here in Colorado?"

Faye set her handbag down next to Toni's keys. The gesture bothered Bo, as if it somehow put her closer to Toni. "I'm here to convince you of your mistake. You weren't answering my calls."

Toni planted her hands on her hips. "This isn't a mistake. This is what I want."

"I know that's what you said, but I'm here to look out for you. I don't think you're thinking clearly about this choice."

Oh yes, she is, Bo thought, itching to step in between Toni and this big-city peacock. *And she's got someone looking out for her.*

"I'm not sure why you're angry with me, but this

isn't the way to show it. You don't really want to do this, do you?" Faye looked around the store as if the place made the absurdity of Toni's choice obvious. "What would make you pull the plug on your career? On what I could give you?"

Toni hands spread in a gesture around the store floor. "You can't give me this. Hearth belongs to you. This is my family's store."

Faye walked down one aisle. The store was overstuffed and in a bit of chaos thanks to the renovation. She picked up a packet of wildflower seeds as if they would burn her fingers.

"You're right. I could give you so much more. I have given you so much more." Faye dismissively tossed the seed packet back into the basket, and Bo felt his gut tighten. "You're so much more than this, Toni. I can make great things happen for you. You know that."

That was it. Bo pushed the sheeting aside again to stand a few feet behind Toni. "Sorry, I forgot to get my keys back. Everything okay out here?"

"Well, isn't he chivalrous?" Faye said with razor-sharp amusement. "We're fine."

Bo clenched his jaw.

"We are *not* fine," Toni fired back. "Faye is leaving."

"But Toni, I've just arrived. Surely—"

Bo stepped closer. "Doesn't sound to me like *my girlfriend* appreciates your presence." He tried to give his words all the edge Faye's glare was giving him.

"No need to get like that." Faye turned to Toni. "Let's talk over lunch."

"Faye, my father's in the hospital. I don't have time for this."

"Dinner, then," Faye pressed. When Toni gave him a look, she said, "I know you don't take time to eat right when you're stressed."

She really wasn't going to leave. "Toni and I have dinner plans, thanks." They didn't, but as far as Bo was concerned, they did now.

"You can postpone dinner with your painter, can't you?"

Bo's gut burned. He put a hand on Toni's elbow. He raised his eyebrow a fraction of an inch and squeezed her arm, a silent signal to follow his lead he knew she'd understand. "I'm not her *painter*," he declared to Faye.

She narrowed her eyes at him. "I don't think you're her boyfriend, either, but let's not get into that now." Faye turned to Toni. "I'll be dining at the little inn across the street. At seven, I imagine. I'm sure hospital visiting hours are over by then. Come by and let's talk this over." With that declaration made, she picked up her handbag, turned on her high heels and walked through the door.

No wonder Toni felt she'd had to clear out of the city. Faye was behaving as if Toni was… How had Toni put it? A pet that wandered off? Bo tried to think of anything to say but came up empty.

Toni slumped against the counter as the door shut behind Faye. She gave a small whimper and let her head fall into one hand. "I didn't think today could get any worse."

Bo wanted to take her in his arms and tell her he'd

make it all okay, but that wasn't the right thing to do. Not now. Instead, he leaned against the counter as well, beside her but careful to keep a respectful distance. "I think you already know this, but I'm sure she means it. She's not going to go back to New York without you. Not any time soon."

"I know. But why?" she moaned.

Because you're worth fighting for, he thought but did not say out loud.

Chapter Ten

An hour later, Toni was home packing some things up for Dad at the hospital and getting the guest room ready for Aunt Roseanne when Marilyn rang the doorbell.

"How is your dad?"

"Okay, sort of. Stable. They're keeping him for two days, maybe longer if they decide to put in a pace-maker."

"Well, maybe the worst of it's over for now," Mari sighed.

"Hardly," Toni admitted. "Give me a hand and I'll tell you about it." While Mari helped her make up the guest-room bed, Toni told her about Faye's surprise appearance.

"You've got to be kidding me!" Marilyn said with wide eyes. "Your old boss is here?"

"She walked into Ed's barbershop not too long after we headed out with the ambulance. As if it's perfectly normal to follow an ex-employee across the country. I knew Faye was extreme, but this?"

"Why is she here?"

"To convince me I've made a horrible mistake and should come back to New York where I belong."

Marilyn's eyes blazed. "I assume you told her to get back on that plane and go home?"

"I tried. Listening isn't one of Faye's stronger skills. She took my leaving very personally. I think I'm the first person who ever quit on her. She's fired everyone else before they got the chance." Toni smoothed the bedspread and set out some towels for her aunt. "She thinks I'm coming to dinner at Gwen's with her tonight so she can set me straight on the evils of following my heart over my career."

"Huh?"

Toni realized her slip. "Bo and I sort of launched an unusual plan earlier." As they walked into her father's bedroom to gather pajamas, a book and some toiletries, Toni told Mari about the fake-relationship selfies. "I actually thought it would convince Faye to leave me alone. Instead, it got her on a plane to come here."

Mari held open a tote bag while Toni put the things inside. "You didn't really think that would work, did you?"

"I couldn't think of anything else that might convince her. A logical argument wasn't working. She's had so many outlandish love affairs, I figured she couldn't argue against it." Toni closed the tote. "Clearly, I was wrong."

"Whose idea were these photos? Yours or Bo's?"

"His. But it's just for show, to help me out. Those were his words, as a matter of fact."

Toni shut her eyes for a moment, fuming at the condescending look in Faye's eyes. *"I'm here to look out for you. I don't think you're thinking clearly about this."* She'd always worked hard to impress Faye, craving her approval. Now it shook Toni's confidence a bit to know how readily her smart and savvy mentor dismissed what she'd done as utter foolishness. *How did I allow myself to let it get so personal? To be so swallowed up by her?* It made Toni more determined to relaunch Redding's and make a success of it. And more annoyed that Faye, who claimed to care about her as the daughter she never had, didn't believe in her.

"So now you and Bo have to keep acting like you're back together to fend Faye off."

It did sound crazy when Mari said it, but Toni was fresh out of other ideas. "Look, I know it's a bit…extreme…but I just want her gone, and this seems like the easiest way to do it. She's always saying how irrational love is, so we'll use that against her. She's certainly not responding rationally to any of the arguments I've used so far."

Mari narrowed her eyes in what Toni thought of as a mom face.

"And you don't think this is a dangerous idea sure to go wrong?"

"I think it's a radical idea for an extreme problem. Faye just needs to see Bo and me together one or two times, and then hopefully she'll retreat back to New York." Toni picked up the tote bag and started down the stairs. "At least that's what I hope will happen."

"I'll say a prayer that this works, and fast." She gave

Toni a concerned look. "And that things don't get complicated in the process."

"They won't," Toni assured. "I've already laid down the law with Bo. We've agreed there's no going back to the way things were between us." Toni tried not to think about all the feelings that cropped up when Bo put his arm around her for those photos. Or what she'd felt when he'd hugged her in the urgent care center. Even if "just for show" wasn't quite accurate, she was home to launch a new life, not resurrect the heartbreak of the old one.

Bo called Toni just before seven that evening to check on things. "I'm heading home," she said, sounding weary. "Visiting hours are over in twenty minutes, and Dad is asleep already anyway."

"Going home with Aunt Roseanne?"

"No, she went back to the house an hour ago. I think she's exhausted from the long trip. I know I'm tired. And hungry. I should have grabbed some food back at the house."

"You're not thinking of meeting Faye for that dinner, are you?" He'd been worried all afternoon that Faye would wear Toni down and get her to agree to the meal. The woman was relentless, and Toni was not in a great place to put up a good resistance.

"Absolutely not."

He was glad to hear that. "Then how does Cuccio's pizza sound? We could take it back to the store and figure out how to work things out while your dad is laid up. Or you can just go home. You need to rest, and the fire alarm issue can totally wait."

"What fire alarm issue?"

Bo wanted to smack his forehead. He hadn't meant to bring that up. "It's nothing. Just a snag we can solve later."

"No, I want to stay on top of things. And it'll give me something to do other than go home and worry. Grab a pizza from Cuccio's and I'll meet you at the store."

Ten minutes later, Bo piled a couple of boxes together as a makeshift table near the store window. A tarp wasn't much of a tablecloth, but this wasn't a date, anyway. He was just looking out for a friend. As he waited for Toni to show up, he stared across the street at the light from the inn's dining room window. Was Faye sitting at Gwen's, waiting for Toni? The hold that woman still seemed to have over Toni worried him. It wasn't hard to see that Faye had somehow filled part of the void left in Toni when her mother died. Now Faye was using that on Toni and trying to control her.

Bo didn't take kindly to that kind of manipulation. Part of him wanted to stomp across the street and give Faye Collins a piece of his mind for trying to talk Toni out of her own dream for Redding's.

But it wasn't his battle to fight. He had no business getting protective over Toni. *So keep me from being a jerk about this, Lord.* Funny how Toni's reappearance in his life had forced him to say that prayer over and over these days.

All thoughts of Faye evaporated the moment Toni walked into the store. Even casually dressed, tired and frayed, she stole his heart. Not in a gussied-up kind of way, but in a deeper, from-the-inside-out way. She wore a T-shirt in the same emerald green as her eyes. Her hair was pulled back in a sensible ponytail, but the way a few tendrils fell down around her neck was beyond distracting. She'd gone from high school pretty to grown-up gorgeous.

It made him wonder how fantastic she would look dressed up for Mari's wedding. And it made him yearn to be there. *Not going to happen*, he had to remind himself. *Boundaries* was starting to become his least favorite word. At least he'd have her friendship—if he didn't screw that up. And the brief appearance of a renewed relationship with her, if not the reality—until Faye left.

As they pulled slices of pizza from the box, Bo watched Toni's gaze wander over toward the inn several times. Maybe setting the meal up near the window wasn't the smartest move. "Do you think she's waiting over there?" Toni asked.

"I'm sure she is," Bo replied. "But hopefully that's where she'll stay. Try not to give her another thought. Maybe she's like a bee—if you ignore her, she'll go away."

"Or she'll sting me." Toni closed her eyes at the first bite of pizza. "Oh, I'd forgotten how good Cuccio's pizza is." After a few bites, she asked, "So what's the problem with the fire alarm?"

"I got the initial inspection back yesterday." Bo hated to show her the estimate from the fire-protection company, but maybe it would provide enough distraction to keep Toni's mind off the dragon lady across the street.

"One Minute" Survey

You get up to **FOUR** books and Mystery Gifts...

See inside for details.

The figure at the bottom of that estimate blew Toni's contingency budget in a single stroke.

Toni cringed and set down her pizza slice. "That much?"

"Or more. I talked them down as low as I could, but once you start making changes this big, they can't grandfather the building codes anymore. You've got to bring this old place up to code."

Toni picked up the paper, the light going out of her eyes as she did. "That's way more than I planned."

Bo sighed. "Welcome to renovation. It's not always a budget-friendly process."

"I was so sure I'd planned for everything. So sure God was clearing the path for me to do this. Then Dad. Then Faye. And now this."

He should have waited for another day to give her this. Why was he always missing the mark with Toni? "These things never go smoothly. There are always unexpected costs. This just happened to be bigger than most."

She swallowed. "That's all the extra money I've got. What if there are more complications?"

There likely would be. But he couldn't bring that up right now. "We'll solve them, too."

Her eyes cut into him. He'd made a promise to her that he'd do whatever it took to rebuild Redding's exactly as she dreamed. "I know you're worried," he reassured her. "But believe me, this is how it goes. For everyone. We can go to the bank together and show them this. Maybe they'll up the loan."

"And if they don't?"

"Then we'll find a place to cut." Bo gave her a strong, steady gaze. "We'll make this work. I promise. You will open on July 3 like you want."

He didn't know whether he had any business making that promise, but his heart was dedicated to the cause. "Let's focus on the good news. The awning looks fabulous at night."

Her eyes lit up. "It glows exactly the way I wanted."

"The right sign says everything. People are already catching on to what you're trying to do. I've heard your word *newfangled* mentioned quite a few times."

"Yeah." She smiled at the awning, almost sighing with happiness. At an awning. That's what made it so hard to blow a hole in her budget like this—the store meant so much to her.

They were partners—well, contractor and customer, technically, but still working together toward the same goal—and it felt like the old Toni and Bo. Things were growing less awkward between them every day. "So I heard the hospital board loved the idea of the fundraiser. I ran into Margaret Washington just outside Cuccio's, and she gushed about your fabulous idea."

Her eyes brightened, and her face softened. "They loved it. We decided to name it Redding's Has Heart and donate 10 percent of the opening's proceeds to the cardiac unit." She picked up her pizza again. "That means a lot to me, given what's happened."

"I'm glad." It didn't matter to him one bit that a charity opening had originally been his idea. He'd been pleased to offer it up, and it was her creativity that would really make it shine.

"Me, too. Good work gets funded, and folks have a great reason to spend money. We have some of the junior volunteers coming over the day after tomorrow to give the bench in front of the store a new coat of red paint."

"I heard. My nephews are going to be there."

"It'll be fun to see you do the Uncle Bo thing."

"You want me there?" He'd hoped to be there but realized he hadn't asked her opinion.

"Of course. You're part of the renovation, after all. It could be good for your business, since Tessa Kennedy is going to take photos and put them in the paper."

That was Toni. Take a good idea and expand it into a dozen great ideas.

Her forehead wrinkled. "Only I don't know if we can still pull it off with everything that's happened."

"Of course you can," he reassured her. "And I'll be there to help. I'll be sure to wear my dress overalls," Bo joked. But his smile disappeared when he caught sight of Faye walking across the street toward the store. This woman did not know when to quit.

"Speaking of fancy clothes," Bo warned as he nodded toward the window. "Your dragon lady's on her way over here."

"I knew it," Toni grumbled. "Grab my hand." She reached across the table.

Nobody needed to tell him twice. *I can't believe I got myself into this.*

Faye knocked on the store door as if she'd been invited. If she saw their linked hands, she didn't acknowledge it when Toni opened the door. "I missed you at dinner. I saw the lights on over here."

"Bo and I were just going over store stuff while grabbing some dinner." She tightened her grip on Bo's hand. "Just like we told you."

Faye stared down at Toni's hand in Bo's. He didn't know if it was intended to make him let go of Toni's hand, but it wasn't going to scare him off. The woman sure knew how to throw shade, he'd give her that much.

"No need to put on a show for my benefit. You can't really expect me to believe that you two just got back together."

Bo wondered if Toni would confess the ruse given that it obviously hadn't worked. That was her call. Instead, she surprised him by keeping her grip on Bo's hand. "I know it may be hard for you to understand this. Bo and I go way back. I suppose it just didn't take long for me to realize what I really wanted. And that's not to be in New York."

Faye turned to Bo. "She's always been a poor liar, hasn't she? It's one of the things I love most about her, actually. Authentic people are hard to come by in New York."

Toni was right—this lady's persistence really did call for desperate measures. He put his arm around Toni and gave Faye a forced grin. "Thanks for stopping by."

Faye smiled right back. "Might we talk, Toni? Alone?"

"Not tonight, Faye. Please just go back to New York. I'm not going to change my mind, and I'm very busy with the store and my dad."

"I'm having some flowers sent to the hospital tomorrow. How is your father?"

"Fine, for now."

There was an awkward moment of silence, and Bo watched Faye lose her hard edge. "Don't shut me out, Toni. I care about you."

It was the first human thing Bo had heard Faye say. The vulnerable words had an effect; he felt Toni's shoulders soften under his arm. Toni had clearly cared about Faye once. And Toni had never been the kind of person who could just shut that off, even when things went sour. *Don't take advantage of Toni's care*, Bo wanted to shout at Faye. *And don't you dare forget I care about her more.*

After another round of Faye trying to extend the conversation and Toni shutting her down, Toni finally watched the door shut behind her former boss.

Faye's words—"Don't shut me out"—echoed straight to Toni's core. She tried to tell herself that it wasn't her problem how the decision to come back to Wander had hurt Faye. Yes, her departure had been fast, but it had needed to be. Even now, even in the midst of her annoyance at how Faye had shown up, Toni could feel the crazy pull Faye had over her. How did she do that?

She was ready for the spiteful "Nobody walks out on me!" version of Faye. This vulnerable, hurt version threw Toni off balance.

"I've never seen this side of her," Toni said as she walked away from the door. "She's really hurt by my leaving."

That brought a flash to Bo's eyes. "You're not seriously defending her, are you? She's convinced she's right. She's trying to tell you you're wrong. As if what you want doesn't matter. She's playing you, Toni."

And there was the old Bo—a blunt instrument, a thrashing reactor. Did she dare mention that what he'd done to her that summer felt just as manipulative? Yes, Bo had opted for brash recklessness rather than vulnerability and hurt, but it had the same motive: to declare she'd made a bad choice and should change her mind and come back to him.

Bo pointed out the window. "She's not leaving. Right there is a woman who will do whatever it takes."

"No, she's probably not packing her bags, much as I wish she were." It was both Faye's most powerful strength and her biggest weakness—once Faye Collins chose a path, there was no diverting her.

Bo grunted. "Oh, believe me, we *will* convince her."

"Any idea how do we do that?"

"We'll figure it out." Bo took her hand again, even though they were out of Faye's sight. "Come on, you know you made the right choice. The new Redding's is going to be amazing. You're supposed to be here."

Bo always seemed to know the right thing to say. He still knew her so well. But that was also what made his outbursts that summer so unforgivable—he had to have known how deeply they would hurt her.

"That's it. We've got to snap you out of this." Bo checked his watch and started pulling her toward the door. "Come on, it'll only take fifteen minutes."

"What?"

"You haven't been on the carousel since you've been back, have you?"

The Wander carousel? Toni didn't see how a ride around Wander's famous merry-go-round would solve anything. No dollar-a-ride turn on any of the carousel's unusual animals would fix Faye or Dad or even Redding's fire alarm system budget. "You're kidding. That's ridiculous."

Now it was Bo's turn to not take no for an answer. "Maybe ridiculous is exactly what you need. Come on, one ride, then you can go home and worry all you want. There's a sheep with your name on it..."

The sheep—Wander's carousel had all kinds of animals but not a single pony—had always been her favorite. Every Wander child—every resident, for that matter—had a favorite.

Why not? It wasn't as if anything else she'd tried lately had worked.

Toni managed a weak laugh as Bo pulled her down the street to the lights of the big red building that housed the indoor carousel. "Okay, but just one ride."

"That's all it usually takes," Bo replied, fishing two dollar bills out of his pocket to hand the volunteer ticket taker.

The carousel's cheerful calliope started up a song as they stepped up onto the platform to select a mount. Toni found the sheep and climbed on, feeling goofy but at least not so tied up in knots. Bo threw his leg over the rhinoceros that stood next to the sheep—his personal favorite—just as the platform began to rotate.

"See what I mean?" he said as Toni laughed. "Some days it's the cure for everything."

A young boy Toni didn't recognize looked at them with puzzled eyes. "Mommy, they're too old for this," he said to the woman holding him on his giant green frog.

"No one's ever too old for the Wander carousel," Toni found herself saying. This, right here, was the heart of Wander Canyon. How did Bo know that the carousel would remind her of everything she loved about this town, about her memories growing up here, and all the reasons she felt out of place in New York?

They ended up riding twice, just because it felt so good after the strain of the last few days. Silly laughter was such a powerful tonic for all the cloudy thinking that had surrounded her. *Thank You, Lord, for this reminder*, Toni thought as they walked back toward Redding's in the dark. *It feels nice to have Bo as a friend again.*

As they reached the Wander Inn Dining Room window, Bo grabbed Toni's elbow. "Uh-oh." He pointed in through the windows, to where Faye sat dining alone. Faye looked up and caught Toni's eye with an expression that was both hurt and hard. The combination gave Toni the distinct impression that Faye wanted her to feel guilty about the choice she'd made.

She felt Bo tug on her elbow. "Just ignore her, Toni. Let's just cross the street so you don't get into round two."

Something hardened in Toni's spine. There would be no round two. If Faye was going to do whatever it took, so could she. It was time to get drastic. It was time to give Faye an irrefutable argument for why she was staying in Wander Canyon.

Without giving it another thought, Toni pulled Bo to the center of the window right in front of where Faye was seated. “Kiss me.”

Chapter Eleven

Kiss her?

Bo's entire body jolted at Toni's request. "Huh?" He practically gulped the word.

Something had warmed between them on the carousel, some carefully packed-away bond that had sprung up in a place where they both had tucked away so many memories. It was all tangling together—the idea to make Faye believe they were reunited, the urge to protect her from everything pulling on her, his own resurrected feelings that were welling up stronger than his own control.

But had she really just asked him to kiss her?

Toni's cheeks flushed, and it made Bo's heart slam against his ribs. She squeezed his hand, tilting her head in the direction where Faye sat on the other side of the restaurant's large front window. "She has to believe that we're a couple, and she doesn't right now. Not yet. I want her on a plane back to New York tomorrow, and if we go all-out, maybe we can make that happen."

Speech felt a bit beyond him at the moment. "You're serious. Kiss you. Here. Now."

Toni evidently mistook his shock for hesitancy, and she pressed on. "I know it's crazy, but you said it yourself. Faye won't stop trying to convince me I've made a mistake. So we've got to convince her."

Toni physically swayed in front of him, as if Faye exerted a magnetic field. Bo's irritation with the woman quadrupled. This wasn't mentorship or guidance, this was control. From the last woman he'd ever expect to allow such control.

Bo realized, at that moment, that he would do anything Toni asked to get her out from under Faye's influence. Anything. Including kissing the living daylights out of her on the sidewalk of Main Street for all to see.

He could do it. Easily. It wasn't as if they'd never kissed before. The challenge would be to kiss her and *not* mean it. Bo wasn't sure that was even possible. It would show, wouldn't it? His true feelings—now roaring up inside—would surely seep through somehow.

And that could be a disaster. It would topple the fragile balance they'd built up, the balance he'd hoped would slowly reconcile their estrangement. A wild leap forward like this—even at her request—might wreck it all.

Or it might not. After all, he owed her, and she'd asked. And he couldn't even put into words how much he wanted to.

So he did.

Bo pulled her to him and kissed her. All the years and all the heartache seemed to melt away in a split second. Of course, it felt stiff and forced—how could it not?—but then there were flashes of closeness. The way those tendrils of her hair feathered against the back of his hand when he slipped his palm against her cheek. The way his lips fit perfectly over hers. She still smelled like wildflowers and sunshine but also something new that fascinated him. When she put her hand on his neck, he was lost, traveling back in time to when they were madly in love. Back when she'd been his heartbeat, the anchor of his wild and reckless spirit. Those glorious days when life spread out before them in pure hope and they hadn't learned how to hurt each other yet.

Bo felt his balance fall away. Literally, because they bumped awkwardly into the restaurant windows midkiss, startling the dozen guests inside. How had he forgotten for even one second that it wasn't just Faye watching? There were people—neighbors and strangers—watching this play out right in front of their eyes. They'd been dining together at the store, they'd been on the carousel together and he'd just kissed Toni Redding in front of a small crowd.

Mortified and flustered, they broke away from each other like high schoolers caught necking by their parents. Bad idea. Really bad idea. What on earth was she thinking to ask that? What was he thinking to do it? His father's words came finger-wagging out of his memory. *The trouble with wanting something too much, son, is that sometimes you get it.*

Now what?

Even if Bo could think of what to say, he didn't dare speak a word. Toni had to call the shots here. He steadied himself and waited for her to speak first.

"Did she see us?"

While Toni's back was to Faye and the window, Bo could catch the woman's scowl out of the corner of his eye. "Oh yeah. Um…actually…everybody saw us."

"Everybody?" She groaned as if she hadn't thought of that. Toni, the consummate planner, was clearly improvising. Did she realize they'd pretty much declared themselves back together? In an indisputably public way? If Wander was always watching, they'd just given the town a front-row seat to their counterfeit reunion.

Only it wasn't all counterfeit. Not for him. Bo couldn't deny that part—most—of the kiss wasn't at all faked. He couldn't bring himself to regret that he had just bulldozed his way across the red line Toni had drawn back in the store cellar. Professional boundaries? There wasn't a shred of that in what he'd just done. Granted, it had been at her request, but none of that changed whatever he'd felt pass between them.

Did she feel it as well? She had to have—it felt enormous. But he was equally sure she wouldn't admit it.

"Why did I just do that?" Toni ducked farther down the sidewalk, away from the window, as if slipping from view would rewind what had just happened. She leaned against the side of the building and squinted her eyes shut.

He followed her. "You wanted to give Faye an argument she couldn't refute. I'm pretty sure you did."

"Not just her. *All of Wander* just saw that."

Not all of Wander—only a dozen or so people—but if the town gossip mill churned as fast as he knew it did, all of Wander would know soon enough. "Maybe that's good. Lots of people will assume we're back together now."

"How is that good?" she moaned.

"That only helps your case with Faye, right?" That was assuming people in Wander would be rooting for this reunion, which wasn't necessarily so.

Bo was just trying to work out what their next step should be when Toni said, "I should just go home now before I come up with any more idiotic suggestions."

My heart is still racing from that last suggestion, Bo thought. "I know you need to get back, but leaving right now might not be the best idea."

She tugged on her ponytail. "And I'm just brimming with good ideas at the moment, aren't I?"

"If we separate now, it'll look like we staged this."

"We *did* stage this."

Bo pulled her toward the store. "We've got to clean things up at the store anyway. Let's go back and take a minute to figure out our next step."

It was an odd role reversal. Toni had always been the planner, the one plotting out next steps, while he had been the directionless wanderer. Now here he was holding her up while she floundered.

"I don't know how she gets under my skin so fast." She cast her eyes back toward the windows as they began walking across the street. "She's my boss, not my mother. How could I have let things get so weird between us?"

Bo wondered if Toni realized how close to the mark her comment was. Could she see as easily as he did how Faye had slipped into that empty space in Toni's life? It wasn't hard to imagine—Toni had adored her mother and had been crushed by the loss. Toni was a woman who loved with her whole heart.

"I've never known you to do anything halfway. Why would your career be anything different?"

She brought one hand up to cover her eyes. He had yet to let go of her other hand. "I am so sorry I kissed you."

He certainly wasn't regretting the last five minutes. "Hey, just for the record, *I* kissed *you*."

"Only because I asked you to."

"Hey, what are friends for? Let's get back to the store, then get you home."

Instead of going straight inside, Toni agreed with Bo's suggestion that they spend a few minutes on the bench under the new Redding's awning. "You're too riled up. Soak in the new glow," he encouraged. "Give things a minute to settle."

Settle? Toni didn't think things would settle any time soon. What had she just done?

Toni half expected Faye to run out of the restaurant after them, chastising her for the silly display and demanding a confession that she and Bo weren't really back together.

Of course that didn't happen, but the confused and overwhelmed sensation in Toni's chest hadn't yet stopped churning. Today—had today really only been a single day?—had left her scattered and flailing. Asking Bo to kiss her? That wasn't any kind of a solution at all. She could live a hundred years and not be able to explain why she'd ever thought that would work to convince Faye to leave her alone.

Still, Bo was right, and sitting under the new awning calmed her. The building somehow seemed to wrap itself around her, the windows and bricks and memories reminding her she ought to be here. The awning, glowing exactly the way she'd envisioned it, helped her to feel like she could make good choices and run a successful store. It felt important to be sitting on the bench that would be repainted tomorrow. She wanted to be heading toward a new future, not dragged back into the past by Faye's inexplicable gravity.

"I think the awning's amazing," Bo remarked. Toni was grateful he sensed she wasn't ready to talk about what had just happened. "It really does glow."

"I had planned to come sit under it tonight, before everything went crazy. But not like this." No, this—whatever this was—wasn't anything close to how she'd hoped today would go.

Suddenly, her cell phone rang in her handbag next to her. The custom ringtone told Toni it was Faye. She didn't answer it. Why hadn't she just blocked Faye's phone number?

Ten seconds later the phone went off again, this time with the "Wedding March." Mari had set it as her designated ringtone as a joke the last time they were together. She made no move to answer her phone this time, either.

"You going answer any of those?" Bo asked as his own phone buzzed in his pocket, an insistent reminder that more people than just Faye had been in Gwen's just now.

"Nope."

"So we're not gonna talk about it?"

Even looking in Bo's direction made her stomach twist at the moment. "Nope." Childish, maybe, but Toni was hanging on by a thread after everything the world had thrown at her today.

"Are you going to start opening the store some nights?"

She was grateful for the change of subject, that he wouldn't push her to talk about what she'd just done. "I want to." Mom and Dad only opened at nights during emergencies or during the holidays. *My Redding's*—she'd come to think of it like that now—*will be open some nights.* People would stop in after dinner or after some town event and just browse around. "Let's go see what's at Redding's," people would say.

She peered down the street, checking again to make sure Faye hadn't followed them.

"I don't know if this is a promise or a threat, but if she has the nerve to come over here, I guarantee you I'll lose my legendary cool." It was a poor joke. Bo's short temper had been his undoing many a time back in the day.

"Okay," he said in reply to the dubious look she gave him. "Bad joke. But I'm kind of scraping the bottom of the barrel given the...circumstances."

"Circumstances?" These circumstances felt like a ten-foot hole she'd just dug and thrown herself inside. It would take her a while to figure out how to dig herself out. They had just kissed. *Kissed.* At her request. In front of a lot of people.

It hadn't been one of her best ideas. But then again, if it actually worked to send Faye away, it'd be worth it. That woman somehow exerted her relentless persuasive pressure any time Toni was near. She knew Toni well enough to press all the right buttons.

Bo's phone went off again in his pocket, and he made no move to retrieve it. "So you're not answering your phone, either?" she asked.

"It's Jake."

"How do you know?"

Bo grimaced. "Because I saw Natalie in the restaurant."

Natalie was Jake's sister. In her mind, Toni could picture texts and phone conversations flying all over Wander Canyon. What had she done?

As Bo ignored yet another call on his phone, he shifted to face her. "I gotta ask. Why did you stay working for someone like her? She strikes me as five kinds of mean and ten kinds of difficult."

Faye had been called far worse. Toni had wondered that very thing lately: Why had she stayed? And why had Faye kept her when she'd fired so many of her predecessors after mere weeks? Toni offered him the best answer she knew so far. "We liked each other."

Bo threw her a dubious glance at that. After all, lots of people respected Faye Collins, but Toni didn't know of too many people who'd claim to *like* her. And for a long time they'd had this odd, beyond-professional affection for each other. It had always been a bit of puzzle to her why they had the connection they did.

"No, really," Toni tried to explain. "I understood her

somehow, if that makes any sense. She made me feel like I was this amazing diamond in the rough, as if she was so proud to discover and hone my talent. It was exciting to have someone like her put so much faith in someone like me."

After a moment—and the *ding* of an incoming text, which she also ignored—Toni added, "I wanted to be someone who belonged in New York, and working for her at Hearth made me feel as if I did." Looking around at the quaint downtown surrounding her, the little stores with potted plants out front and hand-lettered signs in the windows or posters advertising next week's church potluck supper, that craving felt vain and misguided now. As if she'd anchored her dreams in all the wrong places.

"So being someone who belonged in Wander, who belonged with me, wasn't enough." Bo's words were quiet and pained.

His wounded statement dug under her skin. It took a moment or two to answer. "We were teenagers in love. Of course I felt like we belonged together." She let out a sigh, turning her gaze away from him. "But Wander felt too small to me back then. I wanted to see if the big wild fancy world could love me, too."

Shame would keep her from ever saying the deeper truth out loud: she'd wanted to see if she could be loved by someone more sophisticated than Bo Carter from little Wander Canyon. *Oh, Lord, how we look for our worth in all the wrong places.*

"Don't tell me she loved you like a daughter, because what I've seen today doesn't look like love. Not at all."

Bo could always ask the questions that cut deep. "I actually think she does love me the way she knows how to love. Faye doesn't love people so much as she tries to own them."

"You can't own people, Toni. You can't make them do what you want."

She ventured a look at him, as if to be reminded he wasn't the dreamy teenage boy who'd never asked her to stay. He'd always been handsome, but the past years had shaved off some of the restlessness in him. He was a steadier, quieter man now.

They were silent for a moment. Some crickets chirped, and two people laughed with each other on the sidewalk outside Ed's barbershop down the block. It was getting late. She picked up her handbag. "I've been gone too long already. I need to get home."

"Toni—" Bo pressed the handbag back down onto the bench gently "—we gotta talk about it."

"I'm sorry I've created a mess." It was all she felt she could safely say. "I'm sorry I made you kiss me" wouldn't cut it by a long shot. After all, he didn't seem nearly as freaked out by what had just happened as she did.

"Well, I won't say things didn't just get…um…complicated, but if you ask me, it's Faye who did the mess-making. Coming out here like this? Acting like your resignation doesn't count? No offense, but if she's as smart as you say she is, then why is she acting like a complete idiot?"

There was—and had been—plenty of acting like a complete idiot to go around. Herself and Faye currently, but Bo had taken his turn at bad behavior that final summer. In fact, Mari and everyone else who called her to pass along Bo's terrible behavior after she'd left had asked her strikingly similar questions. *Did you hear what Bo did? All the dates with wild girls? The drinking? How could you have been in love with a jerk like that?*

She'd no more been able to understand Bo's epic downward spiral that summer than she did Faye's behavior now.

Maybe it was time to deal with that. Toni plucked a geranium leaf from the pot sitting next to the bench and twirled it between two fingers. "You know, what you did when I ended things with you and left town wasn't much smarter."

She wasn't surprised he took a long moment to reply. "I know." He met her eyes. "But at least I wised up enough to realize that."

"Why, Bo? Why did you do all those things?"

Bo was still for a long time before he sat back on the bench and slowly stretched his long legs out in front of him. "I don't know that there is an explanation. I just sort of came apart. Lost my bearings." There was such an edge of pain to his eyes when he turned his face to her. "I was ready to spend the rest of my life with you, and you yanked that right out from under me."

Toni hadn't counted on the pain in his voice getting to her as much as it did. "We talked about it. You said you supported me reaching for my dreams."

He waved an exasperated hand in the air. "*Of course* I was going to say that. You had already made up your mind. You were going to leave no matter what. What was the point in saying 'don't leave' or 'I need you to stay'?"

A little corner of her heart came undone at his pain. She thought of his words just a moment ago: *You can't own people, Toni. You can't make them do what you want.*

Bo shifted as if his vulnerable words made his skin itch, sitting up to rest his elbows on his knees. He looking down at the sidewalk as if it wasn't possible to say the next words while looking at her. "You broke my heart into a million pieces. I suppose I exploded all over the place to prove you were right to leave me behind."

Bo's words pressed so hard into her it was challenge to breathe. A month ago she would have agreed with them, harsh as they sounded. Now, they just added to the tangle of doubts and second-guessing she was trying to wade through.

She *had* broken his heart. She knew that. But the scorched landscape he'd made in her absence wasn't her fault. He'd told everyone it was, and far too many people did put some of the blame on her. Not too many people thought highly of the girl who left one of Wander's favorite sons behind and reduced him to a pile of poor judgment. She'd heard the phrase *So now you're too good for Wander Canyon and Bo Carter?* more times than she ever expected.

"I'm not sorry I went to New York." She was sorry it was having all these complicated consequences, but those years were not a mistake. Any more than her coming back was the mistake Faye seemed to think it was.

“Anything else you’re sorry for? Lately, I mean?”

He was opening the door wide for her to raise the subject of how she felt about the kiss. She wasn’t going to do it. She wasn’t ready. Oh, they were both thinking about it. The kiss had felt forced, and weird, and a remembered kind of wonderful. But it would never happen again.

Toni picked her handbag back up. “I’m sorry I’ve left Aunt Roseanne alone this long. Do what you can without me tomorrow. I expect I’ll be at the hospital most of the day.”

“Don’t avoid me, Toni. Let’s talk this through.”

She stood up. “Nothing to talk about.”

He stood up, as well. “Come on, Toni. Half the town will be talking about it by tomorrow.”

“I’ve got more important things to worry about than town gossip. And Faye can stick around as long as she wants and it won’t change my mind.”

“Toni…”

“Good night, Bo. Thanks for the pizza.” She stopped short of saying “for everything,” because that felt too weird. “I’ll try and stop in tomorrow.” With that, she walked off toward her car, leaving Bo standing under the silvery glow of Redding’s new awning.

Chapter Twelve

Bo stood under the awning as he watched Toni's car drive away. He tried to pull his thoughts together. They'd kissed. He nearly shook his head at the thought. Lots of people would assume they were back together now, but she hadn't even felt comfortable enough to touch his hand when she said goodbye. So now what? It all felt completely mixed up, as if neither one of them knew how to behave in private given their new public behavior.

And there was no denying it was public knowledge. Bo's phone had gone off in his pocket six times while he was sitting with Toni. Nat had probably been on the phone to Jake before Bo and Toni even stepped off the sidewalk. Peggy probably knew right now, too. And that wasn't even counting the multiple times he'd heard Toni's phone buzzing in her handbag, as well.

Keeping a secret in Wander had always been a challenge. Handing Wander Canyon a juicy topic of gossip in what amounted to a public display? That was a social nightmare.

And he'd just thrown himself on the sword of Toni's request. Willingly. Happily, if he was honest.

His ringtone went off yet again as he stood there. "Enough already," he barked into it.

"Tell me Nat is hallucinating," Jake groaned.

"What did she tell you?" It was a pointless question, but Bo asked it anyway.

"That you two were on the carousel earlier tonight. And that you were just seen kissing outside Gwen's."

There was no point in denying it. "I might have been."

Bo wouldn't have thought you could actually hear someone slap their forehead with their hand over the phone. "You didn't."

He gave the only defense he had. "Well, she asked."

"Do I even want to know why you went from staged photos to carousel rides and kissing on demand?"

Bo gave the shortest account he could manage of Faye's surprise appearance at the store and her rather obsessive pursuit of Toni. "This lady doesn't seem to take no for an answer."

"I can understand the carousel, sort of. But you expect me to believe Toni *made you* kiss her? Out of the blue? To ward off her old boss?"

It sounded even stranger the way Jake described it. "Yeah."

"Because..." Jake cued dubiously. Because she'd asked and he'd been glad to do it. The fact that it broke his heart wide-open to want her back even more probably shouldn't come into the picture.

"I expect she wanted to give Faye a hint she couldn't ignore."

"She gave this lady a hint *nobody* could ignore. It works in your favor if you want her back, but it's kind of an extreme tactic, isn't it?"

Extreme, absurd, dangerous, wonderful. Bo could look up two dozen words for that kiss and not come close to an accurate description. "This lady is beyond extreme. She's got Toni spooked. She seems to have a pull over her that really worries me. I know she's told me and everyone else she came back to take over the store, but I think a huge part of getting out of New York was to get out from underneath this woman's influence. It's like Toni has a stalker in high heels or something."

"Oh, so you were just kissing her for own protection."

"Don't, Jake. Please."

"At the risk of sounding like a fifth grader, how was it? Kissing her after all this time?"

Bo wasn't going to have that conversation. "She asked, I did it. And now it's incredibly weird between us, but we'll get beyond it. And who knows? Maybe it will work and Faye will get back on a plane to New York tomorrow and we can get on with our lives." The moment the words left his mouth, Bo knew just getting on with their lives now was impossible. They'd still have to deal with the fallout from that kiss even if Faye was on her way to the airport at this very minute.

Jake knew it, too. "Where do you think you live,

buddy? You kissed your high school sweetheart in front of a dozen people. Everybody will know. Everybody probably already knows." After a pause Jake added, "I wouldn't be surprised if your folks hear about it."

Mom and Dad—in spite of how much they loved him, or maybe even because of it—wouldn't be in favor of him reuniting with Toni. They'd fear he was just headed for another brokenhearted derailment. If he delayed his trip to Florida for any reason now, they'd lay it at Toni's feet and think she was unraveling his life all over again. And they wouldn't be entirely wrong.

"So people will gab for a few days and it'll die down when someone sees something new to yap about. Maybe Wyatt Walker will do something gossip-worthy at his bachelor party."

Jake would not be deterred. "So what happened after?"

"Nothing. We sat in front of the store for a while."

"And kissed a little more? That bench used to see a lot of action between the two of you back in the day."

Bo was going to have to find some more mature friends. "No." He slumped down on the bench. "We talked. I tried to talk to her about the kiss, but we mostly ended up talking about our history. I told her she broke my heart. And she let me know I failed to make her feel...whatever it was she needed to feel. It was a memorable conversation."

"Ouch."

Yeah, ouch. Kissing Toni had been amazing, but there was so much murky water under their mutual bridge that he couldn't call the episode one way or another. Had they taken one step forward or two steps back?

"Where is she now?"

"She's right here, with her head on my shoulder, listening to our whole conversation."

"No way."

He hoped Jake could hear the eye roll he was giving him. "Of course not. She was already late to get home to her aunt. She was a mess, and I was just trying to get her though this disaster of a day." Bo looked up at the awning glowing over his head. Today had spun so far out of control from the celebration it was supposed to be. Who could blame Toni for not thinking clearly under these circumstances?

He could have—*should* have—been the clear head. He could have declined, advising her that kissing to ward off Faye wasn't a solid plan. *Yeah, right. You couldn't have refused that request for all the world.*

"So now what?"

Jake had a nasty habit of asking that question at times when Bo had no answer. "We get back at work on the store and pray Faye is on the first flight back to New York. Toni will be at the hospital most of tomorrow, and I'll just try and keep my head down at the store." At that moment he squinted his eyes shut as he remembered something. "Until Wednesday."

"What's Wednesday?"

"You know I told you Toni is turning the opening into a fundraiser for the hospital? Margaret Washington is bringing some volunteer kids from Summit by Wednesday. Tessa Kennedy's going to take photos of them painting the bench out front."

Promotionally, it was a great idea—except for the

fact that it included Margaret Washington. If Wander Canyon's gossip wheel had a hub, Margaret was it. Odds of this dying down just went from slim to none.

"You're still up?" Toni was surprised to see Aunt Roseanne sitting at the kitchen table in her bathrobe with a cup of tea and a slice of some delicious-looking pie. Clearly the Wander Community Church food brigade had already swung into action.

"I'm wiped out, but I couldn't sleep knowing one of Katey Ralton's pies was in the fridge." Her aunt got up and began plating a slice of cherry pie for Toni without even asking. "And honestly, I was a bit worried about where you were. Visiting hours were over at seven," she said as she set the plate down in front of the chair across the table. "You okay?"

Where to begin answering that question? "It's been a long day." She took a seat in front of the plate, suddenly feeling twice as weary.

Roseanne patted her hand. "Your father's going to be okay. He's made of tough stuff. Even if they do have to give him a pacemaker, I doubt that will keep Don down for long."

Toni could only nod. Today had scared her deeply. The thought that she might not have many years left with her father nipped at her like an angry bear. Mom's death had hit her hard, and she wasn't at all ready to be an orphan. Could you even be an orphan at twenty-four? *Absolutely*, her panicked heart declared.

"So," Aunt Roseanne started as she carefully paired

a forkful of cherry pie with a bit of the ice cream beside it on the plate. "Pizza and the carousel with Bo Carter."

Toni's mouth fell open. "Seriously?"

"I do still have lots of friends here. And everybody's got a cell phone these days." She gave Toni a serious look. "But Bo?"

That was the million-dollar question, wasn't it? How much did Roseanne know? How much should Toni admit to her?

"He's being a good friend, helping me fix up the store." It was a true statement, but she knew it was only the tip of a big-and-growing-bigger-by-the-minute iceberg.

Aunt Roseanne ate her bite and raised an eyebrow. "I have lots of good friends, too, but none of them kiss me in front of Gwen's."

Toni slumped back in the chair. "So everybody knows."

"'Fraid so." After a pause, Roseanne added, "Didn't you want them to? That wasn't exactly a private kiss."

It was intended for an audience, just not *this wide* an audience. "I wasn't really thinking at the time."

Roseanne chuckled. "Oh, I suspect not. Especially after the day you've had. Just promise me you'll be careful. Things got so tangled between you and Bo before. Maybe now's not the time to move fast on something like that. You're different people now."

"We are." It was true. The person she'd been when she first went to New York might have run back to Hearth when Faye called. That younger Toni would have never found the strength to leave Hearth in the first place. And that person wouldn't have been here to step in and take over Redding's like she was doing now. Toni felt as if she were on an ordained path—most of the time. Cascades of doubts and fears still washed over her, especially when Faye pushed her buttons. So what if people talked? So what if Roseanne and others felt it a mistake to be back with Bo? It wasn't a perfect plan, or maybe even the smartest one, but if the display sent Faye packing, it was worth it.

Tuesday afternoon, after logging a full day at the store, Bo tried to ignore the looks Peggy was giving him as they sat in the baseball field bleachers cheering on Peggy's sons in a Little League game.

"Good swing, Robby," Bo called as the ball swerved off into foul territory. "You got a piece of it." Even though Jake had been the baseball star, Bo had enough skills to pass along batting tips to his nephews. The Car-San logo on the sleeve of the team jerseys always made Bo swell with pride. He'd said an immediate yes when the boys asked if Uncle Bo could sponsor their team.

"Eye on the ball, Robby!" Peggy called to her son, then quietly said, "Not everyone's keeping their eye on the ball these days. What's going on, Bo? Why are you back with her?"

"It just sort of happened." That was true. It just wasn't the whole truth. "We're still figuring it out." That was definitely true. He had no idea how this was all going to play out.

"I get that you both have history, but this fast? She's been back, what, ten days?"

Bo ignored her question and merely called, "There

we go!" as Robby got a solid hit and ran to first base. "Robby on first!" His other nephew, Brian, was batting later in the lineup.

"I still don't even understand why you took the job with her when you're supposed to be heading down to Mom and Dad's as soon as you can."

This was the question he'd been avoiding. Logistically, he could shift the timing for that trip any number of ways. Only Peggy would see any delay as putting Toni before his own parents. He'd been up half the night last night trying to figure out some way to work it out so he wouldn't have to choose between Toni and his folks. No solution had come to him yet. After all, he couldn't very well put off his own parents' needs while admiring Toni for coming to her father's aid now, could he?

He gave Peggy the answer he'd been telling himself. "She's on a fast timetable. We're shooting to have the whole thing done by July 3, and that'll only delay Mom and Dad a bit." That, of course, didn't address the growing reluctance he was feeling about leaving at all. Wander Canyon had been his home. Now that Toni was back, it called to him with more strength. Bo clapped as Robby slid into second on a hit from his teammate. "Way to go, Robby!"

"You're putting a lot on the line to take up with her again." Some days he was grateful for the way Peggy mothered him. Today wasn't one of them. "You don't do short flings, Bo. This won't end well."

"I told you to let me work this out on my own."

"That was before you kissed her while the whole world was watching. She's not good for you, Bo. I don't think that's any less true now than it was six years ago. How much more proof to you need that your sense goes flying out the window around her?"

Bo couldn't really argue with that statement. No sensible man would have done most of the things he'd done with Toni since her return. But sense didn't come into play where his heart and Toni were concerned. And a mountain of logic still couldn't refute how he had never stopped feeling she was the woman for him. *I want to believe You've brought her back to me, Lord. Am I wrong?*

He didn't have an answer. Yet.

Chapter Thirteen

Wednesday morning would have been challenging on a good night's sleep. It was impossible on the tiny amount Toni had managed to get the last two nights. Dad had come home yesterday afternoon, and that was a good thing. Aunt Roseanne was taking great care of him so that Toni could keep today's event at the store happening. The doctors had ultimately chosen not to put in the pacemaker, but there were a whole new batch of medicines to take and issues to watch out for. Still, every time he wheezed or looked unsteady, Toni's heart froze. Was Dad really fine? Or just fine *for now*?

The distance of yesterday's full day at the hospital helped to tamp down the unsettling sensation she felt at even the thought of Bo since Monday. She stayed all day at Summit Community Hospital with Roseanne and Dad, understanding future treatments and options, seeing Dad through final tests, and calming his frustrations over wanting to be home more quickly.

There was also the occasional wink or "How's Bo?"

comment from some Wander resident—many of them worked at the hospital—about what had happened in front of Gwen's. Toni brushed them off as best she could. If anyone had said anything to Dad, he wasn't revealing it. Getting him home was best for everyone, and Toni had breathed a huge sigh of relief last night as she watched him settle into his favorite recliner with a slice of pie and his normal smile.

Dad's smile was just about the only thing normal about her current life. She certainly couldn't call whatever it was happening between her and Bo normal. Something was simmering between them, and she found herself helpless to know if it was just the echo of old history or the spark of some new connection. Six years apart had changed both of them. Every logical instinct told her staying friends with him would be wiser and safer. But ever since they had posed for that first set of photos, there was a constant hum under her skin that refused to die down.

Of course, the kiss had just made everything worse. She could never explain what had led her to that foolish choice. Even the old Hearth saying—"Faye makes people nuts"—didn't seem to sufficiently explain the extreme course of action she'd taken. Desperation wasn't just the mother of invention, it was the mother of bad ideas. *Really* bad ideas.

Hopefully, in this case, it was a really bad idea that actually worked.

Not that she could be sure. Faye had indeed sent flowers to Dad's hospital room, but that neither meant she was leaving nor staying. Faye had called Toni's cell phone four times yesterday, but Toni deleted each voice mail without listening to them.

"Radio silence!" she'd lectured herself in the bathroom mirror before leaving the house yesterday and today. "The way to render Faye useless is to ignore her. The only news you want to hear from that woman is that she's back in New York." She told herself if she made it through today's promotion, she'd consider herself close to home free on this whole crazy week.

Toni had made sure she arrived at the store first this morning, wanting to get everything ready before Bo's truck pulled up. She hated the way her stomach flipped rebelliously at the sight of him. He carried a box from the home supply store in his hand with a set of foam cups balanced on top. Truth be told, the only thing unattractive about him was the weary expression he wore. Evidently, he hadn't gotten much more sleep than she had. It was unfair how mussed looked good on him, whereas she felt nowhere near ready for today's photo shoot.

"Tricky day ahead," he said as he set the box and the two blissfully large coffees from The Depot between them. He'd texted her several updates on renovations over the course of the day yesterday, but this was the first time they'd talked since their conversation on the bench—the same bench that was about to be repainted by the volunteer kids. "Have you figured out how you want to play this?"

She did appreciate that he was letting her the lead on this. It was her store, after all. Only she wasn't sure what to do. She wasn't sure which unsettled her more—what she'd asked Bo to do or how exquisitely he'd managed to do it. Or how easily half the town assumed they'd reunited for real. "Not yet." She grabbed the coffee and drank to keep from answering.

He scratched his chin and stated the obvious. "Everybody knows."

"Maybe it won't matter, since it'll all be over once we're sure Faye has gone back. Then we can admit what this was and just get on with things." What was this, exactly? And what would getting on look like?

He gave an unreadable shrug. "Like you said, desperate times."

They both took a long sip of coffee. "So *is* she gone?" Bo asked.

"I hope so. She left a slew of voice mails yesterday, but I haven't listened to any of them. I called a friend from Heath and told her to let me know when Faye showed back up in the office."

"Ignore bullies and they go away." Bo rubbed his eyes. What Faye was doing was tantamount to bullying, wasn't it? The thought steeled Toni's resolve to dig her heels in and fight for her choices.

"We've still got to figure out what to do about everyone else, at least for today. Well, maybe more specifically Margaret," Bo went on.

Margaret. Toni couldn't have picked a worse person to be scheduled to show up at the store today. Maybe the fact that she'd be surrounded by kids could work in their favor. "We just stay focused on the store."

Bo set his coffee down. "*We* could. But I don't think *she* will." He took two cans of red paint and a dozen small paintbrushes out of the box and checked his watch. "Just muddle through, I suppose."

That plan worked…almost.

"Aren't they adorable?" Margaret crooned over the cute shots of kids in oversize scrub shirts from the hospital serving as smocks while they gave the bench an enthusiastic new coat of red paint. "Get in there on that shot, Toni."

Toni picked up a brush and gave her best smile as the camera began clicking.

"Where are you, Uncle Bo?" Toni secretly wondered if Margaret had called Bo's two nephews to be in on this shot to ensure his appearance. "Come paint with us."

Bo tried to politely decline, but Margaret wasn't having any of it. "Of course you need to be in this shot, too."

"Not really," Bo protested.

"Not from what I've heard. Robby, go get your uncle and make him stand right beside you next to Miss Toni." Subtlety had never been Margaret Washington's strong suit.

Robby dragged his uncle by the elbow to plant him right next to Toni in the shot. "Like this?"

"Exactly. After all, we all know there's more than just a store under reconstruction in this project. Go ahead and put your arm around Toni, Bo." Margaret kept it up until they posed for the camera. A chorus of cutesy kidding came up from the little painters as Bo put his arm around Toni. Toni felt her cheeks redden.

"I'm sure the kids just want to get the painting done

and head over to get their cookies at the bakery," Bo said after Tessa clicked half a dozen more shots.

"Not when these great big cupcakes are coming to them."

Toni turned to see the alarming sight of none other than Faye coming down the street with a giant box from the Wander Canyon Bakery. Bo's arm instinctively tightened around her. *No. Please, God, I prayed so hard for her to leave.*

Faye opened the box to show a dozen enormous cupcakes, which sent the kids dropping their paintbrushes to dash in her direction.

"And who's this?" Margaret asked, far too intrigued.

Toni was preparing to answer when Faye walked over and extended an elegant hand. "Faye Collins. Toni works for me in New York."

Works? Toni's teeth ground at Faye's use of the present tense. They hadn't made any progress at all.

"You've got to be kidding me," Bo said, just loud enough for Toni to hear.

Even over the fluster of the kids choosing their cupcakes, Toni broke away from Bo's arm to walk up to Faye. "I'm so surprised to see you. I was *sure* you were headed back to New York today, Faye." Toni wasn't sure where she found the polite astonishment in her voice. But she was glad it was drowning out the other voice in her head shouting, "Why are you still here?"

"I happened to hear about your little event this morning, and I thought I'd make time to pitch in and help."

She'd love to know how she found out, but Margaret didn't give Toni time to ask. Instead, she motioned for Tessa to get shots of Faye handing out cupcakes.

Bo stepped up to Faye. "Mighty nice of you to find the time *on your way out of town.*" Toni wondered if anyone else caught the edge in his voice. If Faye did, she didn't show it.

"You're leaving us so soon, Ms. Collins?" Margaret asked.

"Faye, please. And no, not quite yet," Faye said, handing a cupcake to the last of the kids. She set down the empty bakery box and reached into her handbag. "Did I make this out correctly?" Toni's mouth nearly fell open as Faye pulled out a check and handed it to Margaret.

Margaret's eyes popped wide. "You most certainly did." She beamed at Toni. "And here I thought New York City didn't have any nice people."

Summit Community Hospital was a great cause and worthy of support, but Toni doubted there was much charity behind what Faye had just done. If it weren't for the kids and Margaret standing right there, Toni might have ripped the check up in front of her for pulling a manipulative stunt like this.

With a huge smile, Margaret turned the check to show Toni. It was for a thousand dollars.

Toni looked at Faye. "I wasn't expecting this." Now there was an understatement.

Faye put a hand to her chest. "I've given a lot of thought to things, and I wanted to support Toni's new project. I ought to be supporting *all* of Toni's new projects."

What was going on with Faye? She was elegant as

usual, but with more of the baffling, lonesome vulnerability Toni had begun to see the other day. Had she finally realized that Toni was leaving her behind? If so, why was she still here?

"I think I'll see to the paint if you don't mind." Bo grumbled, starting to walk off.

"Oh, please don't, Bo," Faye called in a sweet voice. She turned to Margaret. "I think it would be a darling shot to get those two in a kiss near the bench. Just like we all saw in front of the restaurant the other night. Love stories always catch the public eye, don't you think?"

Toni's conscience stung. *You're teaching me a lesson about deception, aren't You, Lord?* "No, I really don't think..."

Margaret clasped her hands with the check still in them. "That's a wonderful idea. Come on, you two, it's for a good cause."

Faye was watching. This was the absolute wrong time and place to go back on their charade now. After all, they'd done it once already, and everybody already knew. It was just for a little bit longer, until Faye cleared out of town. Toni gave Bo an "I'm sorry about this" look and held out her hand toward him.

"If I hadn't already donated, this shot might send me running to my checkbook," Faye said as Tessa raised her camera.

Bo took Toni's hand and stepped closer to her behind the freshly painted red bench. His eyes gave her a look that could have meant a dozen different things as he leaned in and gave her a kiss. It only lasted a second or two, but the swift kiss still felt as if it tilted the sidewalk underneath her feet. The clicks of Tessa's camera sounded too much like a dozen shovels digging her deeper into the hole she'd made.

"Ew, Uncle Bo," young Brian moaned.

"Get back to me in a few years," Bo replied, "and we'll see if you still think that."

Margaret slipped the large check into her handbag with satisfaction glowing on her face. "I do like the way you think," she commented to Faye. "I'm sorry to hear you're on your way out of town."

"To tell you the truth, Margaret, I'm not quite sure about that." Faye had the nerve to make it sound as if the length of her visit was up to Toni. As if Toni's decision to leave New York City and come home to Wander Canyon—not to mention all the blatant requests to Faye that she leave—had never happened. "I was hoping to see a bit more of this store that's been such a big part of Toni's life. I'm in retail, you know."

"Well, you can't leave Wander without seeing Redding's," Margaret said. "It's as much of a Wander institution as our carousel."

"Oh, you gotta go there," a young boy from the group of children piped up. "They have all kinds of crazy animals."

Each of the kids began to chime in with their recommendation for the animals Faye ought to ride. While Toni was considering the unlikelihood of Faye ever riding the carousel, without warning her memory brought up how Bo had asked her to the homecoming dance while seated on the Wander carousel bluebird. He'd given her a wondrous kiss when she'd said yes, and she'd lost her heart to him then and there.

"There's no need, Faye," Toni countered. "You've seen everything there is to see until the renovation is complete. I wouldn't want you to delay your trip on my account. I know Hearth is lost without you at the helm." She wasn't eager to be giving the woman any more tours of the place. "We've gotten all the photos we need, and everyone has finished their cupcakes, so all you kids can head back with Mrs. Washington. I'm sure everyone has a very busy day."

Margaret complied, rounding up sticky-fingered children while saying an enthusiastic goodbye to Faye, with an unfortunate invitation to "Come on back to Wander whenever the notion strikes you!"

When the crowd of little painters had gone, Toni squared her shoulders at Faye. "Let's talk inside." Bo promptly picked up the painting supplies and fell in step behind them.

"Bo, you can start in on the back wall. I'll join you after I finish talking with Faye over here." She put all the command she could into her voice, determined to finish this thing with Faye right now.

Bo gave Toni an "are you sure?" look. When she nodded, he pushed his way through the plastic sheeting and set his toolbox down with a large clang that Toni was sure was meant to broadcast that he was right there if she needed him.

Toni turned to Faye. "What was that all about?"

"A donation to your fundraiser."

As if it really were that simple. Toni pulled in a big

breath to cut straight to the point, even though she thought she'd been rather direct already, more than once. "I appreciate your great big check, Faye, but I can't be bought. I'd have thought you would know that by now."

Faye set down her handbag. "Well, of course I know that. It's one of the things I like most about you. But I wasn't kidding when I said I gave this a lot of thought." Faye peered inside a box on the counter and picked up one of the paper bags Toni had ordered with the new Redding's logo on it. "This is very good, by the way. It hits just the right note."

Faye was brilliant at marketing and never gave false praise. Some small part of Toni could still be pleased that Faye found the logo well designed. "Thank you."

Faye set the bag down again. "Look," Faye said softly, "I don't know what's behind all this. I don't get your sudden rush to come back here when you were climbing so fast at Hearth. You've gotten mixed up somehow. I'm very worried about you—and it's more than just professional. I've decided it's best I stay right here in Wander until we figure it out."

"Faye..." How on earth could this woman still think she should stay?

Faye touched Toni's arm. "And your young man? I'm not sure I understand where all this is coming from."

"I don't expect you to understand." Actually, Toni did. Faye was savvy and logical about everything but romance. The woman's love life was one dramatic disaster after another. Faye Collins, of all people, should have swallowed love as the reason to do just about anything.

Toni picked up Faye's handbag and handed it to her. "Faye, I don't know how else to say this. Please leave. Go back to New York. I'm not coming back to Hearth. Ever."

"You should. You owe yourself so much more than… *this*." To Toni's shock, Faye's voice broke. She had never seen Faye tear up before. "I've invested too much in you for you to end up in just some little shop in the middle of nowhere. And I'm prepared to wait until you figure out that you deserve more."

It was sad and sweet and frustrating all at the same time. Did Faye even realize that this dramatic plea only strengthened Toni's resolve not to go back? To be her own person and not get lost in Faye's intense orbit ever again?

Toni walked over and opened the store door. "You'll be waiting a very long time. Because I won't change my mind. Thank you for everything you've done for me, but please go home. If you insist on waiting for what won't ever happen, don't do it here."

Faye stared at her for a long moment. Then she silently took the handbag from Toni and walked out the open door. As she watched Faye's slow steps across the street, Toni doubted that would be the end of it. She knew Faye well enough to know she never gave up easily.

Faye never gave up, period.

Bo watched Faye walk back across the street from the shop window and had one thought: *I have to get Toni away from her.* He'd done his best not to eavesdrop on Toni's conversation, but the tones of both women's voices were enough to ignite his fear that Faye would find a way. She'd keep on going until she somehow got her hooks back into Toni and lured her back to New York. *How can I help her, Lord? How can I protect her without stepping over the line?*

The prayer made him cringe—hadn't he already stepped over too many lines? He could have stood up to Faye and Margaret, refusing to kiss her for that photo the same way he ought to have refused to kiss her in front of Gwen's, but he'd been powerless to do so. That quick, gentle kiss just now had dug so far into his heart that he didn't care if all of Wander put them back together again. All the reasons why it wasn't wise meant nothing in light of the softness of her cheek and the mesmerizing scent of her.

Stop that. Solution...find a solution that helps her. Thankfully, he hit on one after a few moments' thought: distance. He had the perfect task to take Toni miles from here for a brief spell and let her head clear. He snapped his toolbox shut and walked back over to the open part of the store, glad to see the morning's counter clerk had arrived.

"You okay, Toni?"

"Yeah." She sounded distracted. Confused.

"That barn wood you wanted to repurpose for the back wall? I found it. Nick Gibson will let us take anything we want from one on his place. It's the right color and everything."

"Great." She wasn't even looking at him.

"What do you say we go out there and take a look at it? Clear everybody's head for an hour or two? Is your dad settled enough that you could do that?" The best thing Bo knew for confusion was to get out under the sky, out into the natural landscape that restored a soul's perspective. It was the gift Wander had that New York couldn't hope to match.

"I suppose," she said, still sounding vague.

Bo tugged on her hand, unnerved by how broadsided she still looked. "Okay, then. Let's get you out of here. It's what we both need."

Chapter Fourteen

Bo drove them out into the open land beyond the outskirts of the canyon. It had to help to be out under the huge Colorado sky. Toni didn't speak on the ride, but that was okay. He knew to let the silence and the expanse help sort out the tangle of her thoughts. He needed it himself.

After a while he ventured a touch to her shoulder. "Hey," he said gently. "Talk to me."

Toni shook her head. She simply rolled down the truck window and let the wind flow across her face and hair. He watched as exhaustion sank her into the seat. Life had put her through the wringer in the last few days, and the urge to protect her, to soothe her ragged spirit, overwhelmed him.

We're not back together, he reminded himself. *I can't just swoop in and play hero if I won't be here forever.*

His sister had not minced words yesterday at the ball game about the corner he was painting himself into with Toni. Mom and Dad were struggling to coordinate house repairs in Florida. His skills, and the fact that he didn't have a family to uproot, put him in the ideal situation to help. Yes, Mom and Dad needed him in Florida for a while, but Bo knew that once he went down there, he'd end up staying. He'd been strongly considering the possibility before Toni's arrival.

Now his emotions were making him feel as if he were being pulled in two directions. Bo could sense himself fraying from the strain.

He wanted Toni back. Badly enough to make a mistake in how he did it. Or why he did it. Or what it might do to Mom and Dad. *What's the solution, Lord? This feels like a lose-lose situation. If we reconcile, I'd want it to be because* You *drew us back together.*

Maybe space was the best gift he could give both of them, despite all the words piling up in his head.

They arrived at Gibson's barn and got out of the truck. Bo pulled a pair of gloves from his back pocket and reached into one of the payload compartments to fetch a second pair for her.

With a pop of clarity, he realized there was only one right prayer here: *Let Your will be done, Lord. Give Toni what You know is best for her. For that matter, guide me to what's best for me.* In a blurt of honesty, he added, *But I'm warning You, You're gonna have to scrape me up off the ground if what's best for her isn't me.*

He handed her the gloves and asked, "How many square feet did you think you wanted?"

"Four hundred is ideal, but two-fifty would do."

Bo motioned toward the barn's dilapidated door. "We can find four hundred in there for sure."

They strode through the tall grass to walk inside. The creaky old building looked like every old barn should look—dust motes swirling though stripes of sunshine, rusty tools, birds' nests and weathered walls. The quiet noises of the place seeped into both of them, soothing the tension of the last days. Bo could always feel his spirit open back up in places like this. Where did you go to do that in all the steel and concrete of New York?

He stepped back and let her take the place in. He knew it would set off a surge of ideas—and that was probably the best medicine for Toni right now. Her brain spinning ideas had always been an amazing thing—he could almost hear her think, see the imagination rushing through her body.

"You're right," she said in something close to a wondrous whisper. "It's the perfect color."

She walked over to one of the stalls and ran her hand down the door hanging nearly off its hinges. It saluted her with a squeaky greeting as she swung it aside, and she smiled. "I hope there are four of these."

The stall doors were the reason he'd thought of this barn in the first place. "There are six," he replied with a smile. Toni grinned like a child told to take a second slice of birthday cake. Emotions echoed through Bo like a heartbeat. *I want her back.*

She peered over the stall wall, pointing toward a corner of the space. "Those pulleys over there. Can we have those?"

"Nick said we can have anything we want. He was going to tear it down. He said he'd much rather it go to Redding's instead." After a pause, he dared to add, "People want you to succeed. They're on your side."

Toni began walking around the barn, picking things up, planning, dreaming. It was almost worse to watch her like this—he was always so drawn to her creativity. She could look at something and see possibilities no one else saw. It made it harder to swallow that she'd once looked at Wander—and him—and not seen enough possibility to keep her here. The new Redding's meant that had changed now, didn't it?

He needed to give himself something to do or his heartbeat was going to drown out his good sense. "Should I get started on the doors?"

Her wide-eyed and enthusiastic "Yes!" practically knocked him over.

It was hard to be practical near her. "Go figure out everything you want and start marking the boards to put into the truck. I'll start taking apart those hinges and load the doors."

Bo was grateful the work cleared his brain—sort of. They spent a satisfying hour working in the old barn, her marking the wood she wanted to take while he dismantled the doors and other hardware. The trouble was, he kept looking away from what he was doing to catch a glimpse of her wandering the barn. On the final door his inattention caught up to him. "Ow!" he yelped as it slipped off its hinge to trap three of his fingers in the gap. Pain shot through his hand, but he couldn't lift the door with one hand trapped.

Toni was by his side in a minute, grunting as they combined forces to lift the door just enough to pull his throbbing fingers from the crack. It hurt worse once his fingers were freed, and Bo winced as he tugged off his gloves. This wasn't the kind of mistake he made often, if ever. Then again, working beside Toni had been taxing his attention in new ways since the first hour.

"Did you break anything?" She took his hand in hers, gently peering at the quickly bruising fingers. Which was more excruciating—the wound or her tender touch?

Bo tested his fingers, gritting his teeth as bolts of pain fired through them. They moved, but they felt like they were on fire. "Don't think so," he replied. Simply because he couldn't think of anything else to do, he stuck them in his mouth.

"Oh, that's useful," she teased. "And hardly sanitary."

"I'm not too worried about germs at the moment," he said, the words garbled by a mouthful of throbbing fingers. "Ow," he repeated, just for emphasis.

She gave him a narrow-eyed "oh, grow up" look. "Have you got anything cold in the truck?"

Bo pulled his fingers from his mouth and shook them, quickly discovering that was a very bad idea. "Ouch—yes. There's one of those break-to-activate ice packs in the glove box. Two, actually. Bring 'em both."

This wasn't how he'd seen this outing going. The whole day hadn't gone according to plan, for that matter. Would the prospect of her playing nursemaid to his aching hand make it better or worse? They'd done it dozens of times as teens. He had a scar on that very hand from a time he'd cut himself fishing and she'd bandaged him up with such tender care he ended up kissing her until he bled onto her shirt.

It had made his heart ache when he had kissed her in front of the restaurant. It had made his heart crack wide-open when he'd kissed her this morning.

He wanted to kiss her again. Every part of him longed to get back to what they'd had. Of course, on some level that wasn't possible—they were different, older people now—but the essentials were still there for him. This morning's kiss was quick and cute, but combined with the one in front of the restaurant, it had undone him. Had it done the same to her? She couldn't have kissed him the way she had and not felt some of the same, right? But how was he supposed to know? He felt as if what they *might be* still gleamed bright and shining despite all the muck of hurt and history. The question was, did she?

I want to say something stupid, he thought as he watched her walk back into the barn with the ice packs in her hands. *This isn't the time. Don't let me ruin this, Lord, I'm begging You.*

"Well," she said, smacking the two bags together to give the whack necessary to activate the cold, "this feels familiar." Their history loaded down the words with meaning. But which meaning, for whom?

Rather than reply, Bo simply held his hand out as she sandwiched it between the two ice packs. The aching in his fingers began to subside quickly. The ache in his chest, not so much. "I'll be okay in a bit," he said, even though right now it felt like he would never be okay again.

They sat for a few minutes, a bit of their old easy silence returning.

* * *

"I need to say something," Bo said after a few minutes of icing down his hand.

"Not about Faye." She knew Bo was holding back a lecture about how Faye was treating her, and she didn't want to hear it.

Bo paused, and Toni watched his jaw clench. "Not about her. About me."

She wasn't expecting that.

He shifted the ice packs. "I was planning on going down—maybe even moving—to Florida at the end of the summer. Mom and Dad need my help to rebuild their house, and it's not as if Peggy and her family can go."

The prospect of Bo leaving Wander had never even entered her mind. Now she—the last person anyone expected—was coming home, and he was leaving. It should have made things easier. It should have taken the unwise prospect of their reunion off the table, but it only made Toni's heart twist at the thought of him being gone.

"Only Jake and Peggy know right now. I'm not telling anyone until I'm sure."

"I thought you'd never leave Wander. Are you sure?" She shouldn't have asked. Was he telling her this so she wouldn't be misled by their kisses?

Bo looked at her for a long moment before saying, "No."

Some part of her had assumed Bo would always be here. She realized, at that moment, that the hollow sensation she felt at the thought of him leaving must be only a dim echo of the bombed-out feeling he'd had when she left. Toni yearned to say, "I'll miss you if you go," but that felt far too dangerous. She stayed silent.

He did as well, for a stretch, and then said quietly, "I botched it with you and me. I know that."

She knew she ought to say something in response to a confession like that, but her brain was too tangled to come up with anything.

"I let you go," he went on, "because I didn't think I had the right to ask you to stay."

She didn't have the right to ask him to stay, either. As her contractor or anything else.

"I loved all of you," Bo went on. "And that had to include the big dreaming part that wanted to prove yourself in New York City."

"We were young," she finally said, and that felt wrong. All the ease they'd ever had between them seemed far out of reach now.

She watched him fight with whatever he wanted to say, as if he couldn't decide to speak or say silent. "I was going to ask you to marry me that night," he said, looking down at the straw strewn about their feet.

The admission stole her breath. "What?"

"I was ready to ask you when you broke things off between us. I'd sold my bike and my stereo and emptied my bank account to buy you—" he shook his head "—the dinkiest engagement ring you'd ever seen. You'd probably need a magnifying glass to find it on your finger." He was trying to make a joke, but it fell far short.

The regret between them felt as wide as the sky. "I didn't know," she managed, barely above a whisper.

"Yeah," he said, looking anywhere but at her. "You didn't know."

They sat in silence for another pause. The breeze and insects of the falling-down barn filled the air around them. The peace of the place wasn't enough to drown out the what-if that pressed down on both of them.

Finally Bo turned to look at her. "What would you have said? If I had gotten up the nerve to ask?"

"Does it matter now?"

"Yeah, it matters."

She owed him the truth. "I loved you."

"That's not an answer."

Toni was surprised at the tears that choked her throat. "I needed to go. I needed to see who I was beyond here."

He looked away. "I knew that, you know. That's why I didn't ask. I was stupid enough to think I loved you too much to ask that of you."

She couldn't bear to leave it at that. She wouldn't have said yes, not then. She hadn't even realized he was thinking marriage. *He loved me that much.* The weight of that seemed so much to bear. Toni tried to think of something—anything—to say that honored how much he had cared for her. "I think I would have asked you to wait for me. Would you have?"

He turned her question back on her. "Does it matter now?"

"Yes, it does." It suddenly seemed to matter a great deal.

Bo got very still, and Toni held her breath. There was so much unsaid between them. Was it better to leave it unsaid than to wander into that raw and fragile territory now?

She got her answer when, after a long silence, Bo pulled his hand from the ice packs, flexed his fingers with a wince and walked toward the truck without a word.

Chapter Fifteen

By Thursday morning the wood floors had been repaired and sanded, Dad's medication seemed to be keeping his heart under control and Toni was taking her aunt for a goodbye coffee at Yvonne's bakery while Dad was enjoying his first morning back at the Wander Canyon Community Church men's Bible study.

"Thank you for everything," Toni said as she paid for two enormous gooey cinnamon rolls and a pair of coffees. "I couldn't have managed without you."

"You're family," Aunt Roseanne said with a smile. "And he's still my baby brother." Her smile widened as they sat down. "I always did like telling him what to do. I'd be lying if I didn't say I enjoy another chance to do it." She added cream to her coffee. "And the food. Our dad always used to say you could tell a church by how it fed people. You still got a mighty fine church there." She slid a finger under the waistband of her pants. "I won't need to eat until at least September."

"We may be able to last until December, what with

all the casseroles and salads in our fridge and freezer," Toni said with a small laugh as she broke a warm, flaky curl off her roll. The scent of the sweet cinnamon and rich coffee soaked into her weary soul. She'd hoped for a simpler, quieter life in Wander, but so far her return had been anything but quiet. Or simple. "Do you think Dad's okay?" she dared to ask.

"Oh, I think he's got loads of good years left in him," Roseanne replied. "Time to enjoy the retirement you've made possible. He's been lonesome since your mama's been gone, and while the store gave him something to do, I think it also gave him a place to hide."

Toni had long thought the same thing. "Dad doesn't know how not to keep busy. Some days I worry I'm taking the store away from him."

Roseanne waved the thought away. "No such thing. You're giving him back a life away from the store. Oh, I agree it might be hard at first." Her aunt leaned in. "You'd best let him putter around the new place a bit at the beginning."

Toni tried to imagine her father poking around the internet kiosks or trying to work the computerized cash register. The thought made her chuckle. "Okay."

"But don't you worry. Don will find his way. Half the men at that Bible study over there are well into retirement. They'll pull him into their doings before you know it. And you'll find your way, too." Digging into her cinnamon roll, Roseanne asked, "Has that lady left you alone yet?"

Toni sat back in her chair. "Finally." She pulled her

cell phone out of her handbag to show the one-word text she had received from Faye late last night. Goodbye.

Roseanne shook her head. "And here I thought Don took the cake for stubbornness."

"I think I was just the first person not to give her whatever she wanted. And I do think she was very hurt by my leaving and took it personally."

"Very personally. It's like your mother used to say—'hurt people hurt people.'"

Wasn't that the truth. Hurt came out in all sorts of unfortunate ways sometimes. Bo had let his hurt over her leaving drive him to a load of hurtful behavior. She'd been hurt by his reaction, and hurt him by cutting off all communication from New York—the whole thing became a cycle of wounding. Now, with him heading down to Florida soon, would this round be about him leaving her? Last night she'd lain awake wondering how hard it was going to be to keep Redding's up and running without Bo. She'd come to think of him as a partner of sorts, and a friend.

A friend who gave exquisite kisses, that was.

His refusal to answer her question in Gibson's barn told her he had closed that chapter. Those exquisite kisses were just to help her out, nothing more. Good thing Faye's departure meant they could end that charade soon.

Yvonne poked her head up from behind the bakery display case. "Hey, Toni, do you want another copy of today's paper?"

The photo. How could she have forgotten for a single second about the store bench painting photo?

Yvonne gave Toni a wry smile as she placed the local paper on the table between Toni and Roseanne, folded open to two photos.

One photo showed all the kids and their paintbrushes working on the bench. It was a sweet shot. But next to it was a photo of Bo kissing Toni behind the bench. She'd never really considered Tessa would run that second shot. She'd seemed to be reluctant to even take the picture.

"Should I be telling my new sister-in-law where to aim the bouquet?" Yvonne said with a wink.

"First the restaurant, now the paper. You sure are in a hurry to let everyone know you and Bo are back together." Roseanne lowered her eyebrows at Toni. "Why haven't you talked to your dad about this?"

"It's not what you think."

Roseanne nodded toward the photograph. "Hmm. Not too many ways to misinterpret a kiss like that."

"No, really," Toni protested. The time had finally come to set the record straight now that Faye was gone. "It was all an act. I thought it would convince Faye to leave me alone if she thought I was…following my heart." The words sounded ridiculous now that she said them out loud. "Not the brightest idea, I know, but at least it worked and Faye is finally headed back to New York. She was saying she wouldn't leave without me, so we had to do something."

"Why don't you want us to know you're together?" Roseanne asked.

"We're not."

"Come on," Roseanne scoffed. "You don't really expect me to swallow that, do you? After all, you hired him—of all people—to work on the store."

Toni had been so flabbergasted that people had believed the first kiss, it stunned her they wouldn't believe the truth when she admitted it. "Because he's good and I wanted to use a local company."

"Well," said Yvonne, "he's local, and it sure looks like he's been keeping you company."

"I mean it," Toni insisted. "It was an act for Faye. We're not really back together."

"Why deny it?" Roseanne asked. "Especially when you two got so public about it?"

"I wasn't really thinking. I was desperate to get Faye out of here, and nothing else was working." She pointed toward the paper. "This photo was Faye's idea."

Yvonne raised an eyebrow. "And the other kiss, the one in front of Gwen's? Was that Faye's idea, too?"

"No," Toni said softly. "That was all me."

Roseanne looked puzzled. "So you're not back with Bo? And you don't want to be?"

Now that was a trickier question. "No," she said slowly. It would help if she sounded a lot more certain than that, but she could no longer hide that she wasn't. And she couldn't say that one reason was because Bo was leaving, because she'd promised not to say anything about it. It was the perfect mirror opposite of her first meeting with Bo—only she'd made him promise not to tell she was staying.

"Forgive me if I say you don't sound very convinced," said Roseanne. "You two were pretty serious."

"That was a long time ago," Toni countered.

"When you're sixty-two, a long time means something totally different."

"I hadn't realized there was so much history," Yvonne offered. "Wyatt mentioned something about you two back in high school. I don't think you should be trying to hide that an old flame has rekindled. It's sweet, if you ask me."

"Nothing is going on between Bo and me," Toni reiterated. How could she even be having this conversation? "Nothing real, that is. Like I said, what you saw was all to convince Faye."

Yvonne smirked at the photo. "What I saw looks pretty convincing to me, too."

Was today going to be a nonstop parade of people making comments about that photo? Faye had always known how to garner press. Toni just wished the woman hadn't decided to garner press for her.

Bo had seen Toni's car parked outside the bakery and waited for her to push through Redding's front door. The look on her face told her what he already knew: the photo of their kiss had run in this morning's paper. The kiss that only reinforced the idea that he and Toni were an item again.

But, as Toni had informed him in a quick text late last night, Faye was finally gone. She'd said goodbye and gone back to New York, thanks to Toni's flat-out demand that she leave yesterday.

So now their charade was no longer needed. Toni would want to tell everyone the truth, and the bubble of closeness—even closeness just for show—was about to pop.

As much as he was glad the woman was finally gone from Toni's life, he was absurdly disappointed for it all to end. There were a dozen reasons why he shouldn't take up with Toni again for real. But not a single one of them convinced the part of his heart that still belonged to her. He wanted her back, even though he knew he was alone in that wish. It had been foolishness from the start to think that he could turn that illusion into something real. *You knew that. You've always known that.*

If he needed any further convincing, the look on Toni's face as she walked through the door told him. He was expecting her to be happy that the whole scheme had worked and that Faye was gone. Instead her brows were furrowed in a regretful, even annoyed look. "Come on, is the thought of being paired with me that bad?" he wanted to say, but kept silent.

Toni held a copy of the paper, and it was clear she didn't find the photo nearly as amusing as Jake had. Or any of the other handful of people who'd nudged him in the ribs with a comment at the hardware store this morning.

Toni set down the paper along with the books of paint samples she'd carried in. They were priming the walls today, and she would be choosing the final colors. Even this should have made her happy—painting the walls meant all the structural upgrades and changes were done and the process of decorating could begin. Instead, today felt like the beginning of the end.

"Good morning," he offered in as cheerful a voice as he could manage. "Happy priming day."

"No one believes me," she moaned.

What was that supposed to mean? "Huh?"

"I was just in the bakery saying goodbye to Aunt Roseanne, and Yvonne showed me the photo."

There was no need to clarify which photo. "I've seen it."

"Everybody's seen it. But now that Faye's gone…"

Bo expected her to say, "We can tell everyone the truth." He didn't expect her to repeat, "No one believes me that we faked this for Faye." The news that she'd wasted no time in declaring their faux relationship over poked at his ribs.

Toni was in work clothes for painting, but he still found her beautiful…and slipping out of his reach. Exasperation filled her features and her tone as she worked her hair into a ponytail. "I told Roseanne and Yvonne it was fake, and over now that Faye was gone. They didn't buy it. They thought I was being coy, or shy about it. I don't know. Maybe neither one of them could believe I'd come up with such a ridiculous idea in the first place."

Funny, he didn't think kissing Toni was such a ridiculous idea. The sharpness of her words stung, even though he had no right to let them.

"So now we're going back on it."

She looked at him. "Of course we're going back on it. She's gone—it worked."

He couldn't stop himself from latching on to the split second of something in her eyes before she said that.

Then it was gone and she said, "We just need to figure out how to set everyone straight."

Bo worked to keep his voice even and casual as he asked, "How do you want to do that?" He started opening a can of primer just to give his hands something to do.

"I don't know. I thought we'd just need to tell people, but if this morning is any indication, that might not be enough. Did anyone say anything to you?"

Oh, he'd heard about it, all right. He'd been the recipient of more than one snarky comment about getting back "his girl," but he had no plans to recount them to Toni. "I got a few comments in the hardware store this morning. I just brushed them off without saying anything until I had a chance to talk to you."

"Everyone believes it."

"Well," he ventured as he started stirring the paint, "we haven't given them any reason not to."

"I can't believe I put myself in this situation. Of all the dumb things Faye Collins has made me do, this tops the list."

Bo knew Toni was just frustrated and emotional right now, but it would have been nice if she'd stop referring to their kisses in such regrettable terms. He didn't regret them at all.

"She's gone. That's the important thing, isn't it?" he reminded her as he poured paint into a roller pan and handed her a brush to tackle the smaller spaces and trim. He had to get her working so she calmed down before they could figure out a plan to come clean about the photo and the kisses. He started walking toward the back wall, where he'd already laid down tarps. "Everything else will work itself out. Once people find out I'm leaving, it'll probably all die down anyway." He thought it best to make his decision to leave sound as if it was still solid. Given everything, it was for the best. But if that was true, why hadn't he called his parents and given them a firm date for his arrival?

Toni followed him, dipping her brush into the can of primer to start painting the edges along one corner of the wall. "So what did people say to you?"

He chose his words carefully. "Jake was his usual idiot self," he replied. "He knows it's not real."

That wasn't exactly true. Jake knew Toni intended it not to be real. Jake also knew Bo didn't share that goal. And he'd given Bo a good talking-to this morning about running headlong into heartache. For all the planning he had done with Jake to transition the business in the fall, Jake now seemed to be in a full-blown campaign to send Bo down to Florida as fast as possible.

"Can you believe Yvonne made some comment about how she ought to tell Mari to throw the wedding bouquet right at me?"

Bo just made a noncommittal noise as his mind brought up the picture of being at Wyatt and Mari's wedding. He'd not been invited, but part of him dared to hope that if things held on long enough, he might need to go with her for appearances' sake. The idea of attending the happy ending of such an unlikely love story—with the woman he'd always thought he would marry—appealed to him. *Stop that*, he lectured himself as he dipped the roller into the pan of primer. *Be glad you got to set things right with Toni as a friend before you left. You can't have more. You let her go then; let yourself go now.*

"That got me thinking," Toni went on in a tone of voice that told Bo her mental gears had started turning. "I need to go to Mari's rehearsal dinner tomorrow—and the wedding—alone. Not with you or anyone as my date. I need to go alone. That should make it clear to everyone."

Logically, it wasn't a bad plan. Showing up without him—when he was here in town and supposedly her beau—would probably go a long way in convincing most people the kisses had been a ruse.

"Good plan," he managed to say as he rolled a wide swath of primer onto the wall. He told himself not to look at her, fearful his eyes would reveal the regret that currently soured in his chest. "I mean, after all, you won't really be alone if your dad's going, right?"

Toni stopped painting. "Oh no." She winced. "Dad's at church. He didn't look at the paper this morning, but you know someone at Bible study is going to show it to him. Even if word of the first thing didn't get back to him, there's no avoiding this."

So it wasn't even a kiss now, it was a *thing*? It sure had been a kiss to him. It wasn't hard to read the clues here. This had never been anything more than what Toni had always said it was: him helping her fix the store and get rid of Faye.

If he was smart, he should call his folks tonight and let them know he'd be down just after the Fourth of July holiday.

Trouble was, there was nothing smart about any of this. And nothing solid at all about his conviction to leave.

When Toni walked over to Wander Canyon Community Church an hour later, she wasn't surprised to find her father sitting on the bench in front of the church with a paper in his hand and a look of concern on his face.

"Something you want to tell me?" he asked.

Might as well dive in. She pointed to the paper. "That wasn't real."

Dad raised an eyebrow. "You want to explain that?"

It had been a mistake not to tell him. She'd kept him in the dark about Faye's visit, and her and Bo's campaign to drive her back to New York, because she knew he would get worked up about it. Now wasn't the time to add any stress into his life. And honestly, she'd never thought it would snowball into the complicated mess it had.

"Let's go home for lunch and I'll explain everything."

"Good idea," Dad said as they walked past the Wander Inn restaurant window where much of this had started. "According to Ed, strange things happen outside the window at Gwen's."

Toni cringed as her father gave her a look that told her he knew about that episode now, too. She waited for him to make a remark, but if he had an opinion about what she'd done, he didn't reveal it.

As they drove home, Toni told her father the whole story of Faye's arrival, her persistent pressure to bring Toni back to New York and the extremes she'd gone to with Bo to send Faye home.

"Well, you've actually done it," was his puzzling reply.

"Done what? Made a good mess of things?"

"Kept a secret in Wander Canyon. From me, if not from everyone else. I have to say, I'm surprised I didn't hear about any of this before now. Seems being away from the store pulls me right out of the thick of things."

Was that regret or relief she heard in his voice?

"I'm sorry, Dad," Toni said as they pulled into the driveway.

"I'm sorry you didn't come to me about it," Dad replied. "I might have helped you come up with a better plan than…well, what you came up with."

Toni sighed as she turned off the ignition. "It was stupid, I know. And now that I'm having to face the music and tell everyone what really happened, no one wants to believe me."

"Well, there is that," Dad replied. "Only it did seem to have worked, so I'll be thankful for that much. I think I'm glad I never met this Faye woman. She sounds like a piece of work."

Dad had never come to New York to visit her when she lived there. He always said it was too hard to leave the store, and that he didn't care for big cities. Toni had regularly come home for visits and called frequently. Dad knew Faye was a demanding boss who gave Toni a lot of amazing opportunities, but never much more than that. Certainly no one could have ever foreseen Faye's appearance in Wander Canyon.

Toni asked the question she should have asked a long time ago. "How do I get out of this, Dad?"

Dad grunted loudly as he opened the car door and

pushed himself up and out of the car seat. "Don't know that I've got an answer for you. Only you oughta ask yourself this—why don't people believe it was made up?"

"What do you mean?"

"Pastor Newton said something in Bible study this morning. The thing about really convincing lies is that there's always a little nugget of truth in them. You lied. With good intentions, I'll give you that, but in my experience, schemes like that never come to any good. The real question, if you ask me, is why did you come up with a notion as far-fetched as that in the first place? There must be some nugget in there. And maybe you ought to give that some thought."

Toni stopped halfway through the front door. "Are you saying I should get back together with Bo?"

Dad shook his head. "I'm not saying that at all. I don't like how he hurt you. But he was heartbroken over you, and you know what your mother always said."

"Hurt people hurt people. Aunt Roseanne said the same thing just this morning."

"Oh, so even she knows—and before I did?" Dad's hurt tone was mostly a tease, but it did remind Toni how she'd messed things up.

"The adjective gives birth to the verb," Toni and her father said at the same time, quoting the woman they'd both loved and lost.

And Mom was absolutely right. People who were hurt lashed out in hurtful ways. Hadn't Faye proved that? The same was true of fear, she thought. People backed into a corner rarely behaved wisely—she was living proof of that this week, wasn't she?

"Now what?" Toni groaned.

"I can't tell you what to do," Dad said.

Toni gave a mournful little laugh. "Of course you can. You're my father."

"And you are a grown woman. Which means I can tell you what I think, but the days of my telling you what to do are pretty much over."

Dad, for all his simplicity, was one of the wisest people Toni had ever known. What had ever possessed her to try to solve the issue of Faye without him? There was a difference between being independent and being alone. She could be independent and still rely on the support and guidance of people around her. People who loved her and wanted the best for her. Wander Canyon was filled with those kinds of people. *Thank You, Lord, for bringing me home to that wisdom.*

Toni gave her father a quick little hug before she said, "Okay, Dad, I'm asking. What do you think?"

"I *think*—" he gave the word an emphasis with a twinkle in his eye "—that you ought to figure out why that idea came to you, and what you really think about it." He stared into her eyes. "What *do* you really think about it?"

Toni felt a dozen different things about it. And her thoughts about it were a tangle of plans that hadn't worked out nearly the way she envisioned. "Dad, I have no idea."

Chapter Sixteen

Bo looked around the store with satisfaction. They were actually not that far behind Toni's original tight schedule. Today the final coat of paint went on Redding's walls. Of course, they'd have to repeat the process on the other side of the store, but that would go much faster.

To his surprise, Bo had learned Toni was right: people simply didn't take their denial of the reunion seriously. He shouldn't have been so pleased at this, but a defiant corner of his heart enjoyed how easily some folks in Wander Canyon put them back together, even after all the past drama. It fed his insistent, irrational belief that they belonged together.

That was why he couldn't drum up a lot of motivation to set people straight. He'd dutifully insisted that it had all been for show, but the people only laughed off his explanation. Could he really blame them? The whole thing really was absurd—no one in their right mind would have actually faked kisses to ward off a persistent ex-boss.

Yeah, well, I haven't been in my right mind since she arrived, he agreed to himself.

The cash register on the other side of the store gave its cheery little *cha-ching*, and Bo thought about how much he would miss that sound. After all, once that side was done, Bo should load up his truck and head south as he'd promised. But for how long? A couple of weeks? A couple of months? Forever?

Peggy had made no secret of what she thought was best. There were small concerns about how Mom and Dad were getting along now. But the older they got, the more concerns would rise up. Watching Toni with her father had only heightened Bo's awareness of the aging process ahead for his parents. And while Peggy's husband's job and her children in school held that family here, construction and remodeling were skills that were needed everywhere. From a practical standpoint, he could move easily. He could even argue the case that a move was profitable—there was more work in Florida thanks to the upswing in tropical storms.

Despite all this, his mind continued to concoct reasons to stay. Mom and Dad weren't in crisis by any stretch. They were younger than Toni's parents, and they still had each other. Life was easier on them down south, even if their house needed serious work after the recent bout of storms. *And I like winter*, he argued with himself as he began to roll the rich buttercream-yellow paint Toni had chosen onto the walls.

When Toni arrived and joined him in the painting, the yearning to stick around only grew stronger. *I don't just like winter, I like winter in the canyon. I like being here. I like being beside her, even just like this.*

Toni seemed preoccupied, not engaging in their usual pleasant chatter. He would have liked to think it was with the same relationship wrestling that filled his thoughts, but it was more likely the upcoming wedding. She was only working half a day today, then heading off with Mari to get things ready for tonight's rehearsal dinner and the rest of the weekend's wedding events. That was probably the reason they worked mostly without talking.

"Are you ready for tonight?" he finally asked in an effort to fill the silence that no longer stretched comfortably between them.

"Yeah. It should be fun."

Not much of a conversation starter. He tried again. "It's at Wyatt's, right?"

"On the back deck of the big house at the ranch."

"Sounds great. I mean, who wouldn't like a big barbecue on the Walkers' ranch?" He could never tell Toni that some part of him selfishly wished Faye hadn't left so that he could continue to play the part of Toni's date through this wedding weekend. She shouldn't know how much he wanted to laugh with friends while holding her hand, to give her quick pecks on the cheek and dance with her like they used to. Despite his every effort to drive them out, a cascade of those wishes filled his head as he worked. *I get the whole "honor thy mother and father" thing, Lord, but I'm gonna need your help to let her go.* He couldn't help but add, *If that's what's really how You want things. You already know what I want. And only You know if it's not what I need.*

More prickly silence stretched between them as they worked. The goal of convincing Faye had been reached. The remodeling was heading toward the finishing line. Was there now nothing of what they'd once been to each other but this fragile, awkward friendship?

"Well," Toni said a couple of hours later as she wiped her hands after she finished painting a door trim, "I need to get going. Lots to do."

Bo couldn't stand how the words came forced and cumbersome between them today. If they had to dismantle the appearance of a romance, couldn't they at least find a way to keep a comfortable friendship? Perhaps the whole ruse would make that impossible. Deceptions always had consequences, even well-intentioned ones.

"Yeah, I'll keep on going here," he said to her, striving to keep his voice light. "I might even get started on the barn-wood wall tonight." *It's not as if I have anywhere to be.*

"Oh no, don't do that," Toni protested quickly. "I mean, you should have your Friday night to yourself."

To myself. That about covers it. Just me and Dodger thinking about what you're doing and how I'm not doing it with you.

"I mean, you probably have lots of other things to do." She hesitated a moment before asking, "Have you decided yet? Are you going to stay down in Florida?"

He should say, "Yes," but he found himself saying, "No."

"Dad is so happy to have me back. I'm sure your folks would feel the same way."

Was she telling him to go? He used to be able to read

Toni so well, and now he second-guessed everything he thought about that woman.

"They could use the help, I guess. And there is a lot of business to be had." Still, he couldn't bring himself to say his visit would be a permanent one. It made so much sense—business sense, personal sense, family sense—to leave, but he could not bring himself to commit to it.

"Who'd have thought you'd be the one to leave and I'd be the one to come back?" She fiddled with her hair as she picked up her things. He wanted to read some optimistic hope of her feelings into the unsettled gesture.

He kept painting. "Yeah, who'd have thought?"

More awkward silence.

"Well, obviously I won't be here tomorrow, with the wedding and all. I'll see you Monday, then."

"Sure. Monday. Have fun tonight."

"I will."

"Okay, then," he replied, failing to make it sound ordinary.

Bo watched Toni walk out the door, pretty sure his heart had just walked out behind her.

As Toni was finishing getting ready for the rehearsal dinner, Dad came in to Toni's bedroom, fussing with his shirt. "I can't get the collar to lie down right."

"Here, let me help." She worked the collar into position, finishing with a tender kiss on her father's cheek. "You look sharp, Dad." He'd never been much for dressing up outside of donning a tie for Sunday morning service, so she'd helped him select a shirt for the party. He looked more like his old self today than he had since her arrival. Maybe the medicines really were all he needed, and life would calm down from here on in.

"How are you?" he asked, sitting down on the bed and patting a spot beside him. "Figured out anything yet? You're gonna get asked plenty tonight, I reckon."

"No, I haven't figured it out." Toni sat next to him. "And, well, there's one more thing I haven't told you. Mostly because no one is supposed to know yet. But Bo is leaving Wander Canyon. He's going down to Florida to be nearer his folks. I think some people know he's going down for a month or so to help them do some rebuilding on their house after the storm, but he told me he'll probably stay down there. Permanently."

"Oh," her father replied. "I suppose that changes things—if you had a certain inclination, that is."

"I don't think I have any inclinations. It all feels too risky. I want to focus on the store, and on you. Bo and I…we're just nostalgia, that's all. This past week tells me we can't seem to do anything without making it complicated. And complications are the last thing I need right now."

"You two always were complicated, I'll grant you that. And you're different people now that you're older." He sighed a bit before adding, "But I will tell you one thing. One thing I probably wouldn't have told you before now."

"What's that, Dad?"

"The store is hard to run alone. Your mom and I were such terrific partners, none of it ever felt beyond us. But without her?" His words caught a bit, and Toni was reminded again how much they both missed her. "Let's just say, I'm glad you're back."

"That's exactly it, Dad. Even if I did want to make it real with Bo—and I'm not saying I do—how can I encourage him stay here when I know how great it was for me to come back to you?"

"I know it sounds like those two things are connected. And in some ways they are. But mostly, I think you have to decide what you want. Maybe what God wants for you. Seems to me, that's the starting point for all the other things."

Toni wanted to flop back on the bed like a moody teenager. "I don't know what I want." Well, actually, she knew what part of her wanted. Part of her wondered if she and Bo really could make a go of it. Part of her knew—as Dad had said—how managing Redding's with Bo's help would be so much better than going it alone. Not as a business partner, but as a friend, a sounding board, and the person who could always guide her to a solution when she needed one.

Still, she wasn't alone. She had Dad to guide her. She had solid retail skills and a crystal-clear vision. She had the bone-deep knowledge that God had brought her back here for both Dad and the store. Wasn't that enough?

A certain incident outside a certain restaurant had lit a bonfire of doubts to that notion, and she'd spent every day since trying to ignore the flames.

"Well," Dad said as he pushed himself off the bed. "Figuring that out is the first step. Only right now, we have a party to get to. How about we just head on over and try to have ourselves a good time?"

Toni got up herself and smoothed her dress. "I like that plan."

Chapter Seventeen

Toni tried to have herself a good time. She really did. The rehearsal dinner was at Wyatt's family ranch, on the back deck, which boasted one of the most beautiful views in all of Wander Canyon. The sunset painted a glorious sky, and laughter and good cheer sparkled in the air just as the stars began to illuminate the night sky.

All that beauty didn't do much to soothe the endless questions she got about her and Bo. Toni explained over and over why she was here without him. She told anyone who asked why the kisses had happened and that the extreme plan had been successful. *Half of them believe me now. That's an improvement.* What hadn't improved was how her regret mounted with each explanation of why she'd come up with such a foolish idea in the first place.

You knew there'd come a time to pay the piper, she told herself. She'd expected the endless explanations to plague her throughout the party. What Toni hadn't expected was how uncomfortable she felt being here without Bo's companionship. Where was that coming from? She'd always planned to come with just her father.

Still, her father's words about how it was hard to run the store alone kept echoing in her mind. When she reminded herself of how faithful God had been to her throughout this journey, Toni could come to a wobbling satisfaction about where she was. She tried to view the simplicity of her solitude as resting as easily around her shoulders as the pretty knitted shawls Mari's mother had made each of her bridesmaids.

"So the whole charade is finally over?" Mari said when she was able to break away from the many well-wishers to stand next to Toni at the far edge of the deck.

"Yes. It's finally over." Toni pulled in a deep breath of the sweet mountain air. Would she ever think of this as ordinary again after her six years breathing city air? "It's funny," she went on. "Bo and I were so sure Faye needed to think I had romantic reasons for coming home. All that 'I'm back with Bo' business we thought—I thought—would convince her. Turns out, what finally got through to her was my standing my ground and telling her in no uncertain terms that it was time to leave me alone."

Mari put her arm around her friend. "Why is it we take so long to have faith that the truth is the best way?"

"I wish I knew. I just want things to settle down so I can open the store on time."

Mari laughed. "Oh, I have no doubt you'll open the store. And be a rousing success doing it. The settling-down part? Something tells me it will be a long time before your life is uncomplicated." Toni watched a smile creep across her friend's face as she leaned in. "Which reminds me. Do you have plans to carry any baby items at the new Redding's?"

Toni looked at her friend in shock. Were she and Wyatt planning to add to their new family that quickly?

"Goodness, not me." Mari laughed when she realized Toni's assumption. "But Uncle-to-be Wyatt is a bit anxious about the whole thing."

"Yvonne's expecting?" Toni looked over and had to admit the town bakery owner did seem to have a particular glow about her. Yet another dose of happiness for new love in the canyon.

"A baby by Thanksgiving," Mari explained. "Won't that be fun?"

"Well, I had hoped to start planning purchases next week for Redding's holiday season. I guess I'll need to make sure there are plenty of baby items. And cousin items," she added, glancing at Mari's girls, who were gleefully walking around with a tray of wedding bell cookies playing junior hostesses. "Too bad Margie and Maddie aren't quite old enough to babysit yet."

"You should have heard the squeals when they found out they were going to have a baby cousin." Mari grinned. "They asked Yvonne for a boy, as if she could choose it like cupcake frosting."

"And...?" While she'd seen enough gender-reveal parties on the internet, Toni knew not every couple chose to learn the sex of their baby before birth.

"Let's just say Grandpa Hank is thrilled to know there will be a third generation of Walker men ready to run Wander Canyon Ranch." Mari planted a defiant hand on one hip. "But I will be sure Margie and Maddie—*and* Grandpa Hank—know a Walker *woman* could handle the job just fine, too."

Both women laughed, and Toni toasted the bride-to-be with her iced tea. "Here's to the newest Walker woman. You and Wyatt are going to have a wonderful life together, I know it."

Mari's smile softened. "There's a wonderful life ahead of you with someone, too. I don't know if it will come sooner or later, but I have a whole lot of faith that it's coming someday."

As Toni looked out over the glory of clouds decorating the canyon, she found she could believe it. This was home. How could happiness help but follow?

Bo had spent the whole afternoon working at Redding's. Without Toni. Rehabbing the store with her felt like an adventure—a complicated, awkward adventure, granted, but one he really wanted to take. After she left today and he tackled tasks alone without her energy beside him, it felt like *work*. He'd left the store at five thirty to go feed and let Dodger out, but somehow he had ended up at the Car-San office. Even with the loyal dog's company, his small home felt cavernous and empty knowing where Toni was. He kept imagining her at that rehearsal dinner at Wander Canyon Ranch, telling people over and over that there had never been anything real between them. Probably laughing about what an extreme tactic they'd chosen to take. Fake kisses to drive off an old boss? Who'd have ever believed it?

But it had been real for him. It wasn't helping that his

heart kept coming up with shreds of reasons why that might not be true. Why she might still care for him but just be afraid to admit it. Why people must have seen something to believe they were together even when he and Toni refuted it. All of that was foolish, of course, considering her last words were encouraging him to make his Florida visit permanent.

Bo growled his frustration, listening to it echo in the empty space. Coming here hadn't been any improvement—this place felt just as empty. The whole canyon would probably feel empty to him tonight.

Bo just stood in the middle of the garage, lost in regret. He thought about the stacks of barn wood back at the store, waiting for their installation. He stared at the tin ceiling tiles, which had been their first collaboration, here in this garage to get cleaned and touched up to return to the alternating pattern he'd invented with Toni. It was supposed to be the first of many great ideas they'd come up with as a team.

He'd started this whole thing to help rebuild Redding's *for* her. The truth was he really wanted to rebuild Redding's *with* her.

Heartbroken over Toni felt like far-too-familiar territory.

I've blown it, Lord. I think I always knew I would. Now what?

Bo was so low in his thoughts tonight that he barely noticed when Jake walked in. It was near full dark when Jake opened the door. How many hours had he been here?

Jake sat down on a nearby bench and stared at Bo.

"I don't suppose I need to ask why you're sitting here in the dark sulking."

Bo was grateful the first words out of Jake's mouth weren't "I told you so," even if it was justified.

"It's over. Everyone knows we were never really together, just putting on a show for Faye's sake. I feel like the whole town is laughing at us. Well, maybe just at me. It's just…it's just a job now."

Jake shook his head. "It was always just a job, buddy. You just forgot that for a while."

He knew that. Or he *should* know that. "She's at that rehearsal dinner right now, without me, telling everyone we aren't together. And I'm here." Bo's shoulders sank with the weight of it all. "I kinda hoped Faye would stick around long enough for me to have to go to the wedding as her date. Stupid and selfish of me, isn't it? I've messed up everything."

Jake sighed. "Some things you just can't get back. And you have to know that's for the best given everything, don't you?"

Bo didn't answer that question. No, he didn't know that it was for the best. "Was I wrong to think I could get her back?" He ran his hand along one of the tin tiles. Toni was beautiful and unique and intricate, just like these tiles. He'd felt doubly drawn to the woman she was now, even though he hadn't thought he could love her more than he did back then. "When she showed up in town, I felt like God took pity on my stomped-on heart and said 'I'm giving you another shot.'"

He looked up at Jake, glad to see only compassion and not judgment in his best friend's eyes. "The first time I didn't do enough. Now I did too much. I should save myself from myself and go to Florida. Only I can't seem to make it happen."

"Don't look at me for advice." Jake sat back against the wall. "I've never been this far gone over a woman. Who knows? I might get as stupid as you when my turn comes."

Bo managed a laugh. "I don't know. I set a pretty high bar."

Jake laughed, as well. "Well, I make it a policy only to partner with overachievers."

"So now what?" Bo asked as he set the tile down.

Jake blew out a breath. "Come on, Bo. You know the answer. You finish the job and stick with the plan."

"How?" Bo urged.

Jake shifted his weight. "Do the thing you set out to do—before you got all twisted up trying to win her back. Help Toni get the store ready for opening. And then you go. That way you keep your word, and you keep your heart from getting shredded all over again."

"Too late." There had been no hope for his heart after that kiss, no hope for sound thinking. He'd happily gone down that trail of heartbreak even knowing what awaited him. Funny how the one thing he could never have denied Toni was the one request he should have refused.

"You've got one last job in Wander Canyon." Jake picked up the tile and returned it to Bo's hands. "So do it, and do it well. You can't *have* her, but you can still *help* her. Maybe the only way you get to love Toni is to serve her. Pour that broken heart of yours into giving her the best work you can, and trust God has better things waiting for you in Florida." Jake paused for a moment, looking impressed. "Wow. That was deep. Didn't know I had it in me."

Bo was just as surprised. Jake was always good for a laugh or a knock, but wisdom? That was a new one. Still, he didn't feel the least bit mendable at the moment. "I don't see how that's possible."

"Since when is God in the possible business? I agree, you're one big sorry pile of impossible at the moment, but I seem to remember the Bible saying something about Him showing up in our weakness."

Bo squinted at his friend. "I'm sorry, who are you and what have you done with Jake Sanders?"

"Maybe I'm just a guy sick of watching his friend suffer." He put a hand on Bo's shoulder. "You are a whole lot of heartbroken when it comes to Toni Redding."

Bo narrowed his eyes at his friend. "I'm not so sure I like the new wiser Jake."

"Get used to it. It'll be coming long-distance after this summer anyhow, right?"

Could he do what Jake suggested? Pour out his heart in service to Toni knowing that might be the only love he got to give? The last thing he'd get to do for her before he launched a new life? Whatever he'd tried so far hadn't done him any good, and cutting off all communication with her would be practically impossible. Maybe this was the way to go?

Bo turned to reach for his toolbox.

"Going home to think it over?" Jake asked.

"No," Bo replied. "I'm going to work."

Jake checked his watch. "It's already past eight."

"You know what they say—it's never too late to do the right thing."

Chapter Eighteen

Bo tapped a piece of the barn wood into place on the store wall, feeling the ache all over his back and shoulders. He'd been at this for a few hours, but he couldn't say Jake's idea had worked.

He'd hoped, as Jake suggested, that some sort of peace would come to him as he built Toni's barn-wood wall. That he'd come to a closure that would let him move to Florida with the peace that he was doing the right thing for everyone involved.

He tried to go about his work tonight with an attitude of service, but it wasn't working. He was sulking. Fuming, actually. The most he'd accomplished was exhausting himself.

Everyone in Wander Canyon was out being happy except him. That wasn't true, of course, but it felt like it. The sensible plans he had made seemed to be unraveling right before his eyes, and the only thing he could do was what he'd been hired to do. Put up barn wood. Be the painter, the plasterer, the carpenter, the whatever. He would take up the crusade of helping Toni reach her dreams with the store, then resign himself to the truth that he wasn't going to be by her side when she did it. The thought made his whole body ache with what could have been.

The smart thing to do would be to give up and go home. It was late—he'd probably hurt himself or make a mistake in his present state. But what was the point? Sleep would be beyond him tonight anyway, and there was still a lot of work to do to get the store ready on time.

Toni had chosen a complicated chevron pattern for the barn-wood wall. Jake had been partially right—if this task brought no peace, at least it was a good way to channel his regret. All that cutting and nailing and whacking pieces into place did help a bit. It was certainly better than wandering around his home or the Car-San office, and it kept him busy enough to squelch any urge to drive by Wander Canyon Ranch and peer in at the happy festivities going on without him. *I have no right to miss it. I wasn't ever invited in the first place. I can't miss what was never mine.*

Out of desperation for a solace that refused to come, Bo had started saying a prayer as he fixed each piece to the wall. He prayed for Toni. For Don. For the memory of Irene that seemed to linger all over the store. For all the people who would come into the new store and launch Toni's new life.

And, every once in a while, he said a prayer for his own aching heart.

It wasn't working. He'd been pounding wood for hours, and his heart still felt as splintered as the old boards.

Late into the night, Bo heard the store door open behind him. He turned to see Toni walk in, still in her clothes from the party. Never once had he seen her and not found her beautiful. Even covered in plaster or paint or mud. But tonight, in a turquoise dress that swirled around her figure and a cloud of white lace shawl, she took his breath away.

"Dad went home early from the party. I went back for a little while after I dropped him off, but somehow I ended up driving by the store to see the awning at night again," she explained. "I saw the lights on." With a cautious smile, she added, "Didn't I tell you to go home?"

He tried to shrug casually. "I did. But I came back. I needed something to do." It wasn't even half the real reason, but he couldn't get into that.

She picked her way among the wood scraps and tools to stand in front of his handiwork. She took a deep breath as she gazed at the design. A childish part of him yearned to hear her praise.

"It's beautiful."

So are you. I wanted to be there with you tonight. "It's turning out nice, isn't it?"

"You listened and gave me exactly what I wanted."

"You deserve that. You know you deserve that. If you don't mind my asking, did Faye listen to you? Did she value your ideas or just see you as… I don't know… some sort of mini Faye?"

Toni laughed at the title. "Some. You'd never know it from how she acted here, would you?"

"You're brilliant at this." He set down the hammer he was holding. "If she couldn't see that enough to let you go to your own career, it seems to me you're way better off without her. It was ridiculous how she came after you like that."

Toni picked up one of the boards. "I know. But there was a small part of me that felt good about how she viewed me as indispensable. New York is full of people who'd stab you in the back the minute you turned, and I guess I liked how far she was willing to go to fight for me."

After everything that had happened, Bo was stunned Toni could still find a way to defend how Faye treated her. "Fight for you? Or fight to keep owning you?"

Her eyes flashed, and Bo regretted the outburst the moment he said it. This is why it would never work between them. The pain between them would always make them say things that should never be said.

"You really want to go there, Bo? Do you really want to have a conversation about what fighting for me ought to look like?"

He ought to just walk out of the store and pretend they'd never been here tonight, but he couldn't. The fireball in his chest wouldn't let him. "No, you're right," he replied. "I didn't fight for you. I'm not like Faye. I failed to chase you halfway across the country and beg you to come home and abandon your dreams."

Suddenly, it all boiled up inside him. What was there left to lose? He was going to say it. Bo decided he was done swallowing the words, and if he was ever going to find the courage to speak them, now was the time.

He faced Toni and looked right into her eyes. "The stupid, brutal truth is that I loved you too much to ask you to stay. Because *that's* love. Maybe what I did—or didn't do—was real love, or respect, or maybe it was just dumb teenage cowardice. But no, I didn't fight for you. I let you leave."

I let you leave. The four words burned in his chest, the exposed truth of them spurring him on to say what he had never yet said. What he was running out of time to say. It was as if the frustration inside him had built with each plank he nailed into the wall. Her wall. The wall he was building as a gift to her. The emotions he'd spent the whole night tamping down roared out of his control. "And you couldn't figure out why I fell apart after you left? Really?"

She didn't reply. She looked at him for a long time, her eyes saying a dozen things he couldn't hope to guess, and then turned toward the door.

Do something. Say something. Don't let it end like this. "Don't pretend you can't see how I don't want to leave for Florida after I finish up here. I don't want to be your friend. Or your contractor. I want to help you make Redding's happen. I want to be…"

Toni turned back toward him.

Don't say it! his sensible self shouted to the part of him ready to lay it all on the line. He shouldn't have raised his voice, but he couldn't keep a lid on it any longer. "How could you ask me to fake what didn't need faking? How could you do that to my heart all over again?"

She stared at him. "You want us back together for real." Why did she have to make it sound like such an impossible idea?

"Yes!" he was shouting now. "Yes, I want us back together. I loved you. I've never loved anyone but you."

It felt like his heart split in two when she didn't reply.

"How can you not know that?" His voice cracked on the words, but he didn't care. "I let you go because I thought that's what I was supposed to do. I went off the deep end when you left because I didn't know how to keep on going without you." He held her gaze, feeling completely broken open. "How could you not know how badly I wanted you to stay?" He sounded so needy it stung. "How badly I don't want to leave now that you're back?"

She put her hand against a nearby ladder as if she needed to steady herself. "Why didn't you ever say so?"

He gave the only answer he had, even knowing how selfish it sounded. "I couldn't believe you didn't know. I mean, you *had* to know. And you still left. How could you go, knowing what you meant to me? You were everything to me, Toni. Everything." Suddenly he was as weak and lost as the morning she'd gone. Here he thought he'd done all this growing and changing. What a joke of pride that was. Just reliving her rejection had reduced him to the pile of poor judgment he'd been that summer.

There was no point in holding back now. "You asked me if I would have waited for you. I would have. I did. I'm still waiting for you."

I'm still waiting for you.

The pain in Bo's words hit her as if every board on the wall had come tumbling down.

His kiss in front of the restaurant had been so wondrous, so powerful, and she'd put it down to nostalgia. She'd told herself he no longer loved her because it made it easier to leave, easier to stay away. She lied to herself that everything he'd done was all his fault, and none of it because of how soundly she'd broken his heart.

Bo hadn't really let her leave. He'd loved her enough not to stop her, and there was a difference. Suddenly Redding's, big as it was, wasn't big enough to hold all the pain and regret between them. How did two people who once knew each other so well miss so much between each other now? He was leaving, he ought to leave, and they were foolish to think they still had a chance.

"You said you were going to Florida." Suddenly that didn't seem like enough of a reason. Was she really ready to let Bo slip from her life a second time? To ignore the voice down deep in her chest that had been telling her those kisses weren't false?

Bo took a step toward her. "I won't go if you don't want me to." There was no posturing, no grand gesture. Just a man's broken heart laid out in all its raw pieces. "Do what I couldn't, Toni. Tell me you don't want me to leave. If it's not true, and you don't feel what I feel, then I'll finish up the store and go. But…" His voice left off.

"What about your folks?"

"I'll figure it out. I don't know how, but I will…if you want me to stay. I think you do, and I want to, but I gotta hear it from you."

All the longing she'd been ignoring, the warm feelings simmering between them when they worked side by side, the way he made her feel strong and confident and on the right path, clamored for her to say *stay*. And yet the word wouldn't come. What right did she have to ask him to drop his plans like that? After sticking to hers and leaving him those long years ago?

"We're different people, but we're still good together. Better. You see that, don't you?" He gestured around the space. "It's all over this place."

Toni looked around and saw Bo's hand was everywhere. Here she thought the new Redding's was all her design, but it wasn't. His presence was in the tin tiles, the artful shelves, the texture of the floorboards, the careful, intricate design of the barn wood on the wall. Every detail of the entire building bore witness to what Bo hadn't said until tonight.

She'd been thinking she'd built the new Redding's all by herself, all for herself. She was so busy cherishing her new independence that she'd been blind to his quiet contributions beside her.

Dad told her it was hard to run the store alone. Maybe she didn't have to. Maybe independence wasn't the same thing as *inter*dependence.

"I still love you, Toni. And if this place is the only way I ever get to show it, then I'll swallow that." He took another step toward her. "But I've got so much more to show you. I want to find a way to stay. To prove to you how we belong together. How we always have. Ask me. Ask me to stay."

She waited for him to close the gap between them, for the intensity of his eyes to become the intensity of his kiss. Only he didn't. This last space was hers to cross. Bo would never, ever make demands on her. The greatest gift she could give him, the balm to heal the wounds of their past, was to choose him now.

The inches between them felt enormous and then again so easily crossed. As if they'd stepped back onto a path they should have never wandered from. Proof again that God's grace could always exceed a soul's mistakes.

"Stay." The intake of breath she heard as she leaned in to kiss him was the sound of a heart becoming whole again. It sounded the way she felt stepping back into Wander.

She felt a tear slide down her cheek as Bo's arms came around her and he said, "I will," with the solemnity of a vow. The embrace was gentle and full of wonder at first, but it quickly took on strength. Bo clung to her fiercely, and in mere seconds she was clinging to him, as well. She held him close, like something treasured and long lost now restored. It wasn't weak or painful anymore—it was true. If the kiss in front of Gwen's had been powerful, this one swept her completely off her feet.

"Well," he said as she laid her head on his shoulder, "that was worth waiting for."

She looked up at him. "Waiting? I just kissed you on Wednesday."

He tightened his arms around her, and Toni felt her body go peaceful for perhaps the first time since she'd come back home. He tipped her chin up to him, and kissed her again.

This kiss was pure joy. Delight and grace and tenderness. All the past years melted into something new, something full of possibility.

"How are we going to do this?" she asked.

"I don't know," he sighed. "But we'll find a way. We'll talk to my folks and Jake and Peggy, and we'll figure it out. There's a load of questions to ask, but at the moment I have the one answer I need."

Toni felt as if the room glowed around them like the awning outside. "Maybe, but I've still got a question."

"What's that?"

"What are you doing tomorrow night?"

He grinned, his arms still tight around her. "I'm kind of busy. This wall isn't gonna finish itself, and there's that last set of cabinets that needs putting up." His eyes sparkled. "Why do you ask?"

"I need a date for a wedding."

He pulled back playfully. "Are you asking me out?"

"Oh," she said, wrapping her arms around his neck and pulling him close again. "I think I just asked for a whole lot more than that."

"Whatever the customer wants..."

Epilogue

It was the middle of the day, but somehow the Redding's awning glowed. Or was it just her? Toni felt as if the whole building glowed as bright as the fireworks that would fill the Wander sky tomorrow night.

Redding's—her Redding's—was finally, fully open.

Red, white and blue bunting adorned the front windows while cheery pinwheels in the same colors peeked out from the planters on either side of the bright red door. A big, beautiful Grand Reopening sign hung out front, and Toni smiled broadly as Tessa Kennedy took a photograph for the paper.

The store was packed. There had been a crowd from the moment she had turned the key in the lock with Dad and Bo beaming right beside her. Friends and neighbors wandered through the new space, chatting, congratulating and making purchases. And no one thought to ask if the embrace Bo gave her as she stepped over the store threshold was real.

Toni felt her grin widening as she rung up the first

sale of the day. She still wasn't sure how Bo had done it, but he'd managed to find someone from the local high school who figured out how to make the new computerized cash register make the *cha-ching* sound she'd loved so much from the old one. It was one of a million small touches Bo had lent to the place as they readied the store for today. She was grateful for every single one of them. And for the second chance to be the person she should have been all along. The old cash register had been given a second life as well, repurposed to hold a collection of handmade silverware and serving pieces from an extraordinary artist just outside the canyon.

Cha-ching. Cha-ching. Cha-ching. If the number of times that sound rang through the store was any indication, Redding's—and by extension Summit Community Hospital—was going to have a very successful day.

"It's gorgeous!" Mari said as she, the twins and Wyatt roamed the sales floor. "I see a dozen things I want. You're about to become my new favorite obsession."

"I thought *I* was your new favorite obsession," Wyatt joked as he kissed his new wife on the cheek. "Are you going to shop here *and* on our honeymoon?" The couple was headed off for a week just after the upcoming holiday.

"You don't know much about girls, do you?" Margie said to her new stepfather as she handed her mother a headband she'd been eyeing. "We shop all the time."

Toni smiled at the sweet little girl. "I'm counting on that." She turned to Wyatt. "Besides, part of everything today goes to the hospital, so it's good-deed shopping."

"Does that mean I can have two?" Margie asked.

Wyatt threw up his hands in defeat. "I'm in way over my head here."

Toni laughed as the new family wandered off in search of more good-deed finds. She laughed and waved at Jake Sanders as he held up a little boy-size T-shirt that said As Handsome as My Uncle, pointing at his sister, Natalie, and his young nephew Cole. This was exactly how she'd pictured the store—wonderful merchandise, happy shoppers, friends stopping by. Not just commerce, but community.

Customers and well-wishers kept her busy, but every once in a while Toni would peer through the crowd to catch Bo's eye. He'd been here all morning, and each time she looked at him, her heart sang at the genuine pride and pleasure in his eyes.

With a twinkle in her own eyes, Toni caught Bo's gaze and raised one eyebrow, inclining her head in the direction of the stockroom. All this commotion was great fun, but she wanted a moment of privacy with the man who had reclaimed her heart.

They kissed once out of sight, and Toni felt dazzled all over again by what had grown back up between them. It was just as familiar and yet as newfangled as the store itself.

"You're a success," he said against her cheek. She could hear the smile in his voice.

"We did it. On time and everything." They'd pulled far too many late nights to make it happen, but Toni found herself glad and grateful to be sharing the load with Bo. It was just like Dad said—hard, but possible with the right partner.

"I love every single thing about the store," Bo said. "I love every single thing about you." For a man who'd kept silent about his feelings when she first came into town, it seemed he couldn't stop declaring them lately.

"I love you, too. Still, and all over again." It had become a saying between them.

Bo grinned like he was up to something. "Which reminds me. When you get a moment, check the piece of barn wood on the left side of the wall. The one with the tiny star in one corner."

"Why?"

"If I told you, it wouldn't be a surprise, would it?"

Intrigued, Toni took his hand and pulled him back out into the store to stand by the wall decorated with the rustic old wood from Gibson's barn. Now, of course, the design was filled with hooks and fixtures that hosted an assortment of items, but she quickly found one small piece on the left side that boasted a little carved star.

"What is this?"

"My dad always told me a good craftsman finds a way to sign his work. This is mine. Slide it out."

Toni tugged a bit on the square of wood, finding it slid out easily. Drawn on the wall underneath, in Bo's precise handwriting, was a red heart with the initials *BC + TR* inside. It looked just like the one they'd inscribed on a tree down by the riverbank back in high school. Only this one had an addition. Below the heart read, *Wait for me.*

He'd be leaving just after the holiday for three weeks down in Florida with his parents. And of course, it would feel like forever, given how inseparable they'd been since the night of Mari's rehearsal dinner. The night they'd rediscovered the love that had never quite left either of their hearts.

But Bo would be back. After long discussions with his parents and Peggy, it was decided that Bo would make quarterly weeklong trips down to Florida to help his parents in whatever way they needed. But his primary business—and his heart—would remain here in Wander Canyon. True to his word, Bo had worked out a plan that honored both his parents and the life he wanted to build with Toni here.

Toni slipped her hand into his. "I will." She would wait. Bo was worth waiting for.

"Still and all over again," he said, eyes glowing with a loyalty she'd come to hold dear. Bo kept his promises. Time and distance would never come between them again. Her heart skipped a beat. Today really did feel like the launch of her forever. There were challenges ahead, to be sure, but just as many blessings.

The fire in his eyes doubled, making her head spin in the most delightful way. "Ask me to kiss you," he said.

Hadn't she just kissed him? "Why?"

"Ask me to kiss you in front of everybody," he added. "It worked so well the last time, we ought to try it again."

Bo was always full of good ideas. "Kiss me in front of everybody."

He did. Still and all over again, now and forever.

* * * * *

If you enjoyed this story, be sure to check out the first book in the Wander Canyon series

Their Wander Canyon Wish

And be sure to pick up Allie Pleiter's previous miniseries Matrimony Valley

His Surprise Son
Snowbound with the Best Man
Wander Canyon Courtship

Find these and other great reads at www.LoveInspired.com

Dear Reader,

Life's choices can take us down paths we never dreamed. When we commit those paths to God's sovereignty, however, we can always trust that they lead to our best futures. That's a hard promise to hold when we feel our choices have tangled our lives into knots, but as Jake Sanders points out, we serve a God who specializes in impossibilities.

I hope Toni and Bo's story gives you hope for the knots in your life. God is the great untangler, and it is my prayer that their happy ending reminds you of what is possible in your future.

If you've grown as fond of Jake Sanders as I have, know that his heart is the next one to find a happy ending in Wander Canyon.

Until then, you can always reach me on Facebook, Twitter or Instagram, or drop me an old-fashioned letter at PO Box 7026, Villa Park, IL 60181.

Blessings,
Allie

COMING NEXT MONTH FROM
Love Inspired

Available May 19, 2020

HER AMISH SUITOR'S SECRET

Amish of Serenity Ridge • by Carrie Lighte

Recently deceived by her ex-fiancé, Amish restaurant owner Rose Allgyer agrees to temporarily manage her uncle's lakeside cabins in Maine. Falling in love again is the last thing she wants—until she meets groundskeeper Caleb Miller. But when she discovers he's hiding something, can she ever trust him with her heart?

THE NANNY'S AMISH FAMILY

Redemption's Amish Legacies • by Patricia Johns

Starting her new schoolteacher job, Patience Flaud didn't expect to help Amish bachelor Thomas Wiebe with the *English* daughter he never knew existed. But as she works with the child to settle her into the Amish way of life, Patience can't help but be drawn to the handsome father and adorable little girl.

STARTING OVER IN TEXAS

Red Dog Ranch • by Jessica Keller

Returning to his family ranch is the fresh start widower Boone Jarrett and his daughter need. But he quickly learns rodeo rider Violet Byrd will challenge his every decision. Now they must find a way to put aside their differences to work together...and possibly become a family.

THE COWBOY'S SACRIFICE

Double R Legacy • by Danica Favorite

Lawyer Ty Warner doesn't quite believe Rachel Henderson's story when the single mother arrives at her long-lost grandfather's ranch. She's hoping he'll connect her with family who might donate the kidney she needs to survive. But when he learns she's telling the truth, he'll do anything to help her.

A MOTHER'S HOMECOMING

by Lisa Carter

Charmed by the two-year-old twins in her toddler tumbling class, Maggie Arledge is shocked to learn they're the children she gave up for adoption. And now sparks are flying between her and Bridger Hollingsworth, the uncle caring for the boys. Can she let herself get attached...and risk exposing secrets from her past?

BUILDING A FAMILY

by Jennifer Slattery

Worried the reckless bull rider she once knew isn't the right person to care for their orphaned niece and nephew, Kayla Fisher heads to her hometown to fight for custody. But Noah Williams is a changed man—and he intends to prove it. Might raising the children together be the perfect solution?

LOOK FOR THESE AND OTHER LOVE INSPIRED BOOKS WHEREVER BOOKS ARE SOLD, INCLUDING MOST BOOKSTORES, SUPERMARKETS, DISCOUNT STORES AND DRUGSTORES.

LICNM0520

USA TODAY **bestselling author**

SHEILA ROBERTS

returns with the next book in her irresistible Moonlight Harbor series, set on the charming Washington coast.

Moira Wellman has always loved makeovers—helping women find their most beautiful selves. Funny how it's taken her five years with her abusive boyfriend, Lang, to realize she needs a life makeover. When Moira finally gets the courage to leave Lang, the beachside town of Moonlight Harbor is the perfect place to start her new life.

Soon Moira is right at home, working as a stylist at Waves Salon, making new friends, saving her clients from beauty blunders and helping the women of Moonlight Harbor find the confidence to take back their lives. When she meets a handsome police officer, she's more than willing to give him a free haircut. Maybe even her heart. But is she really ready for romance after Lang? And what if her new friend is in hot pursuit of that same cop? This is worse than a bad perm. Life surely can't get any more difficult. Or can it?

With all the heart and humor readers have come to expect from a Sheila Roberts novel, *Beachside Beginnings* is the story of one woman finding the courage to live her best life. And where better to live it than at the beach?

Coming soon from MIRA books.

Be sure to connect with us at:

Harlequin.com/Newsletters

Facebook.com/HarlequinBooks

Twitter.com/HarlequinBooks

Harlequin.com

MSR089

SPECIAL EXCERPT FROM

Join USA TODAY *bestselling author Sheila Roberts for a seaside escape to the beaches of Moonlight Harbor.*

Arlene had left and Pearl had just finished trimming Jo's hair when the bell over the door of Waves Salon jingled and in walked Edie Patterson followed by a woman, who was the image of young and hip, holding a cat carrier.

"Whoa," said Jo, looking at her.

Whoa was right. The girl wore the latest style in jeans. Her jacket and gray sweater, while not high-end quality, were equally stylish. She had a tiny gold hoop threaded through one nostril, and when she flipped her hair aside part of a butterfly tattoo showed on her neck. Her features were pretty and her makeup beautifully done. And that hair. She had glorious hair—long, shimmery and luminescent like a pearl or the inside of an oyster shell. The colors were magical.

This had to be the woman Michael had sent down. Either that or she was a gift from the hair gods. She looked around the salon, taking it all in.

Pearl saw the flash of disappointment in her eyes and suddenly knew how exposed Adam and Eve must have felt after they ate that forbidden fruit. *Adam, we're naked!* Looking at her little salon through the newcomer's eyes, she saw all the things that had become invisible to her over the years: the pink shampoo bowls, old Formica styling stations, posters on the walls showing dated hairstyles like mullets and feathered bangs. The walls were the same dull cream color they'd been when Pearl had first bought the place. And the ancient linoleum floor…ugh. The place looked tired and old. With the exception of Chastity and Tyrella Lamb, who was getting her nails done, so did the women in it.

MEXPSR089